STAR BOUNTY

RICK PARTLOW

aethonbooks.com

ALSO IN STAR BOUNTY

Absolution

Retribution

Revolution

[1]

THE DOG LOOKED at me with earnest, soulful brown eyes and his left ear cocked upward curiously.

"You're not going to fuck this up again like last time, are you?" he asked.

I favored him with a scowl and nodded toward the airlock hatch.

"Shut up and get in character," I told him. He leered at me and whoofed with fake cheerfulness.

The indicators went green and the outer airlock door of the *Charietto* opened into the barely-contained chaos of El Mercado. People rushed by, mostly because staying in one place too long meant having to fend off the obnoxiously aggressive street vendors, and the beggars and the pickpockets who worked in conjunction with them. I rested my right palm on my holstered blaster and stepped out into the madness.

The wave of sound and smell and color crashed over us, overwhelming. Rainbow hair, skin merely a tapestry for holographic tattoos, clothes as colorful and ostentatious as possible to hide the fact they were cheaply-fabricated flash. It was all a cynical attempt at camouflage, trying to hide their poverty and desperation from anyone stupid enough to dock at El Mercado without knowing what it was and who lived here.

If the Panicle was the heart of the Epsilon Indi system, then El Mercado was the rot at its core. Men and women came to the Panicle to seek their fortunes in the asteroid mines or in selling their wares and services to those who did, and the refuse, the failures, the misfits all seemed to wash out into El Mercado. The only good thing I could say about the place was it had artificial gravity. Docking on one of the stations in the Paragon out at Barnard's Star usually meant dealing with zero-gee in the docking bays. The older stations still used rotation for centripetal force, built before the development of gravity generators, and I had to put up with incipient motion sickness every time we docked at their non-spinning hubs.

Dog thought it was hilarious, of course.

"Mister!" a kid with dreadlocks animated into Medusa-like snakes using miniature actuators rushed up to me, holding a cloth sewn with pockets, each carrying a different plastic syrette. "You want buy Kick? Zero? Sting? I got all the good drugs."

He couldn't have been older than twelve.

"Where's your mom and dad, kid?" I asked him, brushing past. "They know you're out here selling drugs to tourists?"

"Where you think I get the drugs, man?" he demanded, raising his arms up, a cloth extended from each hand as I walked away. "Hey, maybe your dog want drugs?"

"It's a sad statement on the human condition," Dog said, shaking his head.

I thought I saw a couple of heads turn, visitors in more expensive clothes, unused to the assault on their senses. Just glances, unsure what they'd thought they'd heard. The locals didn't even spare Dog a glance, just went about their jobs.

"I told you to shut up," I reminded him, pushing a beggar

aside with a sweep of my forearm, then grimacing as I realized he'd gotten something slimy on the sleeve of my jacket.

Real leather, too, damn it.

I leaned down and wiped it against Dog's side and he snarled at me.

"I saw that," he growled a warning.

"Good. See more, talk less."

I bypassed the train station. Most newcomers used it because the map menus were simple and they definitely didn't want to get lost in the wrong section of El Mercado. *As if there's a* right *section.* I knew where I was going and I wanted to attract less attention on the way there. We walked.

There was no customs inspection, no passport control. Anyone could bring pretty much anything into El Mercado except nuclear, biological or chemical weapons. At least, that's what the official rules said, and I assumed they had remote detectors for that sort of thing. They certainly had no problems with guns, because just about every third or fourth person I saw was carrying one openly, and I had to assume the others had them concealed.

No issues with robots, either, though I didn't see as many of those. Dog didn't get a second look once he stopped talking. Robots were the toys of the rich or the tools of heavy industry, and El Mercado had very few of the first and none of the second. The heavy industry was in the asteroid belt a few million kilometers away. The entertainment and business and housing for the heavy industry was closer, just a few kilometers off to either side in the other districts of the massive Panicle station. El Mercado was everything else, the things people didn't want to admit they wanted.

Drugs were ubiquitous, the labs where they were made squatting in solitary ugliness, wrapped in protective fencing and insulation, guarded by men and women with guns. They watched us pass, not caring who we were or what our business was as long as we weren't a threat. They sold in the streets, in stalls crammed into niches and corners, in fancy storefronts catering to the wealthier visitors. Guns were sold as openly, though their quality varied. Old-fashioned slug-shooters fabricated off patterns centuries old were spread across blankets on the ground on street corners, while blasters like the one I carried were restricted to storefronts, protected behind thick polyglass shields and watched over by an armed sales staff.

The rest was harder to spot. Illegal and black-market virtual reality software, pirated fabricator patterns, even Bartoli crystals, although those were the most jealously guarded of all, kept in safes and carried out to ships or businesses by escorts. Nothing was marked, nothing was advertised. If you were there, you knew what you meant to shop for and where to find it.

I was looking for sex. Sex was everywhere, and like everything else here, for sale. Live companionship was available, but expensive. Once, there'd been actual human trafficking in places like this, but the Marshals hadn't tolerated it for long. Prostitution was legal, pimping was not, and any attempt by a house to take more than a fifty percent cut of companion's income was met by law enforcement raids, and no one here wanted that, particularly when the clientele for real, human companions tended to be wealthy.

Most lonely people tended not to be wealthy, which was why pleasure doll rental was a thing, though here they tried to get fancy and call themselves Lifestyle Companionship Providers. You could call it whatever you wanted, but the bottom line was, you were having sex with a robot, and a not too bright one at that.

Security was pretty stiff, no pun intended, at the live, human brothels. Not so much at the robot version. Their main concern was that none of the drunken spacers who stopped by tried to steal one of the dolls and take it with them on their ship for entertainment. At least not without paying for it.

The place I was looking for had a sign in bright, neon orange that advertised "Live Robot Sex," as if they didn't see the oxymoron inherent in the term, right beneath the imaginative name of the place: "Congress with the Beast." Most of their clientele was probably too drunk to care. Dog and I walked past an unconscious asteroid miner with a plastic jug of whiskey in one hand and his pants around his ankles and through the front door. A woman sat at the front desk, her expression a statement on boredom painted by one of the old masters. She didn't bother with the holographic tattoos or the dyed skin or robotic hair weaves, just let her utter lack of interest be her camouflage.

"Hi, I'm Nikki, welcome to Congress with the Beast." The words were as rote as if they'd been read from a script, her eyes as dead as any of the pleasure dolls'. Then she saw Dog and one of her eyebrows shot up and I finally noticed actual interest. "We don't usually allow pets," she said, although I sensed a "but" coming involving extra payment for an exception.

"He's a robot," I told her, pulling a wad of paper trade notes from my jacket and slipping a few extra in with the advertised amount. "I find he enhances the experience for me, if you know what I mean."

"Whatever floats your boat, cowboy," she said with a shrug, stuffing the cash into the back pocket of her ratty jeans. "No weapons in the back though." She gestured toward my blaster. "You'll have to leave that in the lockers along with anything else you might be carrying. No use trying to sneak it through, we got a scanner."

The scanner was rudimentary, a plastic halo over the doorway into the hall, and I wondered if it even worked. There were three dozen lockers in the reception area, rusted and battered metal, painted a puke green a million years ago and faded nearly to white now. Each had a thumbprint reader to secure it, and I chose one in the middle at eye level and stashed the gun inside it, peeled off a glove and let it read my print. I entrusted the number on the front to memory, then paused and looked at Dog.

"Record," I told him. "Remember 12B. End record."

Which was a show for Nikki, since Dog had probably already taken it upon himself to remember the locker number, if for no other reason than to rub it in my face if I forgot it.

"You know, cowboy," Nikki said, her voice low and conspiratorial, as if there were anyone else in the room or anyone at all who cared, "if you want, I could probably get you a first-class AI for your dog there. I could fix him up good, get him to where he could fly your ship and have real conversations and even work as your bodyguard."

"It's pretty damn illegal to install that kind of AI in a robot without a license," I told her. She rolled her eyes and made a rude gesture with her hand. "Anyway," I went on, eyeing Dog significantly, "who the hell would want a dog that talks all the time?"

Dog's right ear tilted at me and he frowned.

"Whatever, buddy," Nikki said. "Your loss. What kind of companionship you looking for today? We got male and female models in all sizes, colors and shapes. If you want anything too wild, it'll take an hour or so and cost more."

I suppressed a disinterested shrug. I couldn't care less, but I didn't want her to realize that.

"Female, skinny, long dark hair."

She nodded and punched those parameters into a menu.

"Right. Room twenty-three." Her voice went back to its original drone, the rote recital she had to give a hundred times a day. "There's a bathroom in there. Once you leave the room, the door's locked and you have to pay again to re-enter. The robot can't leave the room and if you try to take her out, an alarm will sound and she'll deactivate, *and* you'll get blacklisted from ever coming here again. We clear?"

"Crystal," I assured her over my shoulder, walking past the desk.

Dog followed at my left heel, tail wagging as if he was looking forward to this.

The hallway was dimly lit, on purpose I was sure. No one wanted to see the faces of the other customers, or have theirs seen. A couple of them passed by us along the way, a wild-haired older man with crazy eyes shining in the dark, his shoulder rubbing against the other wall to keep his balance. Alcohol wafted off of him, the smell strong enough to make me want to heave. The other was a woman, broad-shouldered and rough looking in work coveralls. She didn't meet my eyes, her stance slightly embarrassed.

I don't know why a female would be any more embarrassed for being there than a man, but humans are funny that way. I didn't say a word, listening to the sounds of my boot soles tapping against the tile, the click-click of Dog's claws in quiet echo. I looked for the numbers on the doors and began seeing odd on the left, even on the right. And right where I expected it, I saw a larger, more reinforced door, metal where the others were plastic, with an ID plate affixed above the knob. The sign at eye-level gave no indication of the room's purpose, just warned customers to stay out.

I made a mental note of its location and kept moving. Twenty-one was another ten meters down and to the left. I tried it and found it open. The knob was grimy, sticky with some substance I wasn't anxious to know the provenance of, and I was glad I'd worn gloves. The door was light and cheap, plastic with sound-proofing insulation glued to the back, more of it on the walls. The bed was basic and uncomfortable looking, but then I guess it wasn't meant to be slept in.

The girl on the bed looked very comfortable. I had to do a double-take when I saw her face, lean and sharp and pale, the dark hair spilling down over one eye. She looked just like Janie, and I wondered if I'd asked for those specifications with her in mind. Probably. I don't have much of an imagination. What she was wearing did *not* remind me of my ex-wife, and I was fairly sure Janie had never even owned something with that much lace and so little in the way of actual covering.

"Come on in, cowboy," the pleasure doll invited, smiling in a way determined by armies of clinical psychologists to guarantee excitement. "Close the door and let's have some fun."

I pushed the door shut.

"Are there cameras in here?" I asked, standing a meter from the bed, arms crossed.

"Do you want there to be cameras?" the doll asked me, her responses cobbled together from a limited range of possibilities. "Do you want someone to watch?"

"Of course there are," Dog answered, knowing he was the one I'd been speaking to. "I've already taken care of them. They really don't even have anything you might call a firewall on these systems. It's almost criminal negligence." He laughed, and if you don't think a human laugh is an odd and unsettling thing coming from something that looks like a cross between an English mastiff and a Labrador retriever, well then, you've never been around Dog.

"Your dog is funny," the doll said, imitating his laugh, which made it somewhere around ten times as weird.

"Shut her up, will you?" I said plaintively, nodding towards the bed.

Dog hopped up on the bed and rested a paw against the pleasure doll's forehead. She froze in place, mouth half-open as she'd prepared to say something else, her limited AI system determined to be seductive no matter what.

"How the heck do people live with themselves?" I wondered aloud, shaking my head.

"Thank God I don't have to find out," Dog said, then presented his hind end to me. "You want this thing or what? It's taking up too much space in my ass."

"You don't have an ass," I reminded him. I slapped him on the rump. "Hand it over."

The compartment opened up above his right rear leg and I reached in and pulled out my backup piece, a more compact, slightly less powerful version of the blaster I'd entrusted to the house weapons lockers. I hoped I'd get that one back. Quality weapons weren't cheap and I had a certain sentimental attachment to it.

The hidden compartment disappeared into Dog's fur as if it had never opened and I tucked the blaster into my jacket pocket. I kept my hand inside the pocket as I pulled the door back open and checked outside. Nothing except a muted grunting from a nearby room with inadequate soundproofing.

"Come on."

It was a short but tense walk back to the door we'd seen. I wasn't worried about their security cameras, not with Dog taking care of it, but a place like this would have bouncers. Human bouncers, I mean. I doubted anyone even in El Mercado would take the risk of programming robots to potentially harm humans. The storm that would bring down on them would be Biblical in its proportions and wouldn't just involve the Marshals. They'd have the damn Navy in here, and not to arrest anyone either.

The ID plate on the door taunted me, daring me to try it. I looked down at Dog, gesturing to the lock.

"Good Lord, what use are you, anyway, Masterson?" he said, raising his head up to the plate, leaning his front paws against the door. He stared at the lock and I saw a laser from his right eye scanning across the plate.

Something clicked and I pushed the handle downward. It opened. I slipped inside and closed it quickly, just giving Dog enough time to squeeze through behind me. The door had opened into a narrow, dark entrance hall that opened up a couple meters down, light dimly filtering from some source in the main room. Rack after rack of spare parts were mounted to the walls, heads, hands, feet, knees, all stripped bare of artificial flesh, the white plastic gleaming bonelike in the muted light.

Work tables were lined up in the center of the room, each occupied by a pleasure doll under repair, some with their flesh in place, others inhuman skeletons laid open, actuator motors and fluid-filled artificial muscles in full view. Maybe there was some deep, philosophical analogy to be made there to our society, beautiful and perfect on the outside but with a profane ugliness just under the surface. I don't know, I'm not that smart.

Neither was the guy leaning over one of the metal worktables, stretching synthetic skin on over the frame of a very well-endowed male robot. Nothing about the man's slack, sallow face screamed "genius" to me, and neither did the fact he'd no sooner broken out of federal custody than he'd run his happy little ass right back to the very last address on his file.

I levelled the blaster at him and waited for him to notice me. And waited. And waited some more. Dog looked at me sidelong and shook his head. He didn't speak, but I got the message.

"You know, Mr. Schiff," I said, "I wish I got along well enough with *my* ex-wife for her to give me a job while I was on the run from the cops."

His head popped up like a prairie dog who'd just spotted a hawk circling, eyes wide, mouth dropping open. He let the robot's skin slip out of his hands and it whipped backwards, smacking him in the face with the pleasure doll's main attraction and leaving a curiously-shaped red mark on his cheek.

"What…," he stammered, hands going up at the sight of the gun. "What do you want?"

I laughed. I couldn't help it. I felt bad, because I try not to laugh at the misfortunes of others, having been there myself, but the utter cluelessness of the man tickled me.

"Abel," I told him gently, "I'm a bounty hunter duly licensed by the Union of Aligned Worlds Law Enforcement Commission to act on their behalf in the apprehension of federal fugitives. Of which you are one, having been charged with hijacking, grand theft, assault with a deadly weapon and attempting to flee across interstellar jurisdictions. I'm here to take you in."

I pulled a flex-cuff out of my pocket and tossed it to him. He caught it by instinct, staring at it with incomprehension.

"Put those on."

The light finally came on behind Schiff's beady, dull-witted eyes and he made a sudden lunge for the door, as if my blaster wouldn't have burned a hole right through him. Or heck, maybe he was smarter than I thought and he knew I wasn't going to shoot him down in cold blood. And I wasn't, but that wasn't my only option.

"Dog," I said.

Dog didn't growl. He *could* growl, and I preferred it when he did because it made him sound more threatening, but he felt it was undignified. Apparently, he didn't see anything undignified about grabbing a man by the testicles and biting down *just* hard enough to prove it could hurt.

Abel Schiff screamed, falling flat on his back and yanking at Dog's fur, as if he could somehow pry him off.

"Please! No! Don't hurt me!"

"He won't hurt you unless I tell him to hurt you," I assured the man. "And I won't tell him to unless you try to run."

I walked over and picked up the flex cuffs from where he'd dropped them.

"Now let's try this again. Get to your feet and put your hands behind your back."

I should have known something would go wrong. This had

been too easy and, while I'd had my share of easy apprehensions before, not a one of them was in El Mercado. So, when we walked out of the repair center and straight into the yawning muzzles of a pair of old-style projectile weapons held in the hands of two very large men who I assumed were bouncers, I wasn't surprised. I also wasn't surprised to see Nikki Cortez standing behind them, fists on her hips and a disgusted look on her face.

"Abel, what the fuck have you gotten yourself into this time, you worthless piece of shit?" she demanded.

I ignored her for a moment and considered the guns. They weren't blasters, weren't any sort of energy weapon. They were short-barreled shotguns and if they were loaded with anti-personnel flechettes or lead shot, my armored jacket might stop them. But if they hit my head, I was going to wind up with my brains splattered all over the wall. I didn't think they'd do Schiff much good either.

"Ms. Cortez," I said, trying to stay calm, my blaster pointed somewhere between the two gunmen, "I am a bounty hunter, duly licensed by…"

"Yeah, I heard all that shit when you said it to this stupid fucker," she cut me off, gesturing at Schiff, who looked quite the sight with his hands behind his back and Dog hanging off his balls. "That don't mean I intend to let you haul my worthless ex-husband's ass out of my place without a fight."

"Don't do it, Nikki!" Schiff pleaded, his face a deathly pale, sweat pouring from his high forehead. "This here dog will rip my testicles off if you shoot him!"

"Shut the hell up, Abel!" she snapped. I got the sense from the look in her eyes that, despite the verbal abuse she was heaping on the man, she actually did still care about him.

"Ms. Cortez," I tried again, "I don't want anyone to get hurt, not you or your men, or your ex-husband and least of all myself."

Dog uttered a low whine, complaining I'd forgotten about him, but I ignored it.

"I know going to jail sucks, but it's not the end of the world. They teach you a trade inside, and try to get you a job when you get out if you're nonviolent and haven't caused trouble during your sentence. Abel here seems like a nice, well-mannered fella, and I'm sure he'll do fine in prison, right Abel?"

"I'll do just fine, Nikki!" Schiff insisted, eyes never leaving Dog's teeth. "Swear to God, I'm looking forward to it!"

"I said shut up, Abel!" she told him, glaring at me.

"I'm being straight with you now, Ms. Cortez," I told her. "I'm a former Marshal, with all the training and skills you might think that brings with it. I can kill both of your men before they squeeze the trigger."

Maybe. I was a fair shot, and the armor would help, but they were really damn close.

"I could do it and get away with it," I went on. "Being how this is El Mercado, I wouldn't even have to report it. But I don't want anyone to get hurt. I'm just doing my job."

Then one of the big boys fucked up. I knew if anyone did, it'd be one of them. They looked ugly as sin and twice as stupid and from the nearly matching scowls on their faces, they were itching to try something whether or not this Nikki woman ordered it. I'll give the guy credit, at least he did it the right way. He didn't talk, didn't start posturing like a mountain gorilla beating his chest. The only sign I had was the muzzle of his shotgun raising slightly as he went for the headshot, the cabled muscles of his forearm tightening as he began to squeeze the trigger. It was enough.

Bear in mind, the way I'd learned to shoot was fairly straight-forward. You aim center mass and fire till the threat is resolved. Nothing tricky, and most of the time it winded up with someone dead. I was trying to avoid that and I had the luxury of standing there for several seconds with a gun in my hand, thinking about ways to avoid it. So, when I saw the hired muscle on the left make his move, I was ready. All it took was a half-step to the side and I fired.

The blaster discharge was a lightning strike in the enclosed hallway, the flash enough to have blinded me if I hadn't already slitted my eyes against it. It burned right through the stamped-metal receiver of the shotgun, splashing the big ape holding it with molten metal. He was halfway to a scream but I was already moving, slamming my shoulder into the chest of the other goon, his shotgun pinned between us as his back impacted the wall. I swung the butt of my blaster into the side of his neck and he dropped, his eyes rolling back into his head.

The other one *was* screaming now, rolling on the ground trying to put out bits of his shirt that had caught on fire with hands scorched black. Schiff was screaming, too, begging Dog not to bite him, while Nikki Cortez was trying to pull a compact handgun out of her pocket. I levelled the blaster at her and shook my head.

"I believe I have demonstrated great restraint," I said, stepping over and kicking the shotgun away from the guard I'd hit. He was coming to, and I didn't want him to get any funny ideas. "I'd appreciate it if you could leave that gun where it is until after we're gone."

She glowered at me, but she pulled her hand out of her pocket. Heads were starting to pop out of open doors now, customers checking on the screaming. I aimed my weapon at the ceiling on the far end of the hall and fired off another round, sending flaming insulation dropping to the floor and touching off a chorus of curses and slamming doors.

"Come on," I grunted to Dog, backing away from Nikki and her two goons, trying to watch them and our avenue of egress. I needed another pair of eyes, but Dog's were buried in Schiff's crotch and don't think I wasn't planning on giving him grief about that for the next several weeks either.

"I'll see you again, cowboy," Nikki Cortez promised, the glare in her eyes as hot and dangerous as a naked nuclear core.

"I doubt it, ma'am," I assured her, pausing beside the gun lockers to peel off a glove with my teeth and use my thumbprint to retrieve my blaster. It slid into the holster with a relieved hiss of metal against leather. "I tend to prefer my female companions breathing and thinking. Maybe my dog might want to come back though." I grinned at him, backing towards the exterior door. "He seems to enjoy the company here."

"Fuck you," Dog remarked around the material of Schiff's pants as we exited. I clucked at him reprovingly.

"Don't talk with your mouth full."

[2]

Government Central was a much more civilized section of the Panicle, sedate and well-organized, with reserved and tasteful signs telling you where to go and what rules you had to follow. No guns here, of course, unless the Marshals carried them, and I certainly didn't bring Dog along. Robots weren't welcome, bounty hunters only slightly less so.

I ignored the glares and dirty looks as I walked Abel Schiff into the Fugitive Recovery Department of the Union of Aligned Worlds Law Enforcement Local Headquarters (Epsilon Indi) past hallways decorated with certificates of recognition and awards of achievement on one side and memorials to the fallen on the other. The blue uniforms were neatly-pressed and spotless, the haircuts all perfectly regulation, and the frosty disdain almost universal.

Bounty hunters were living proof the Marshals weren't perfect, that they *didn't* always get the bad guys and needed help from the unwashed, barely-regulated scum of the galaxy. And I was a step *below* that.

A tall, broad-shouldered senior Marshal with blond hair buzzed down to his scalp was coming down the corridor from the lobby with a shorter, slimmer, younger officer to his right and he made a point to bang his shoulder into mine.

"You should watch your step," the blond growled at me, lip curling with disgust. He snorted a humorless laugh and spoke to the man next to him loud enough so everyone in the room ahead and the hallway behind could hear. "You know, Junior Inspector Calvert, you'd think a man might be smart enough not to keep coming back where he's not wanted."

I brushed past him, not bothering to respond. No use giving the asshole exactly what he wanted.

"What's with him?" Schiff asked me, whispering. "What's he got against you?"

"I used to work here," I admitted.

Schiff stared at him in obvious disbelief.

"But you seem like an all-right dude," he said, "except for the whole arresting me thing. These guys are dicks."

"I'm sure they're nice to their families." I pulled open a door and guided the fugitive through it. "Here we are."

"Another one?" the matronly woman behind the counter asked, grinning when she saw me stepping up with Schiff in tow. "Don't you ever sleep?"

"I got ship payments to make, Gracie," I told her, smiling for the first time since I'd entered the facility. Gracie was a civilian employee despite her blue uniform, and just about the only friendly face in the building. "Meet my good friend Abel Schiff, wanted for hijacking, assault and grand theft."

I took out a multi-tool and snapped the flex cuffs off Schiff's wrists, then nodded toward the ID screen mounted on Gracie's desk.

"Do I gotta?" he asked in a plaintive whine. "I mean, is there some technicality where if I don't volunteer my ID, you have to let me go? Or something?"

Gracie rolled her eyes at me. "Is he serious?"

Schiff seemed hurt by the comment and I'd kind of grown fond of the little guy so I put a supporting hand on his shoulder.

"Look at it this way, Abel," I told him, "the quickest way out of prison for you is good behavior. This isn't like the local jails you've been in where they're more interested in how big of a fine your relatives can pay them to get you out early. The feds love well-behaved, non-violent prisoners. It can knock as much as half your sentence right off the back end. So, why not start now and get in practice?"

Schiff seemed to consider the concept for a few seconds before he put his palm against the ID pad. The holographic readout projected above it confirmed his identity, the list of crimes and, most importantly to me, the reward.

"Well, there you go," Gracie said, slapping the counter in satisfaction. She touched a button to activate the intercom. "I need two officers to Fugitive Recovery for a transfer, please."

"When you get to your long-term holding facility," I said to Abel, trying to sound serious to get his attention, "the first thing you need to remember is *keep your mouth shut*. Just keep your head down, do your time and don't mouth off to anyone, not the guards, not other prisoners, no matter how much they deserve it. It might feel good when you do it, but it will bite you in the ass. Second thing is, don't get involved. The guards aren't your friends, the prisoners aren't your friends, so don't expect them to be. You see someone getting pushed around, just turn and walk the other way. Your only concern is getting out of there as quick as possible."

Schiff was nodding when the two uniformed officers came for him. They quickly and efficiently put him into neural restraints and marched him off toward processing. He didn't say anything— he couldn't with the neural web in place—but I thought I saw gratitude in his eyes. Unless that was fear.

"Wow, that's some great advice you gave him." The voice

came from just over my right shoulder, and should have startled me, but I'd smelled him coming. Larry fancied himself a player and wore just a bit too much cologne. "Not bitter or anything, are we?"

Larry Daniels was looming behind me, arms across his chest, looking down from his towering two meters with a glower of disapproval. He had one of those faces, too good looking to be a cop but not quite as good looking as he thought, and he wore his brown hair at the very edge of regulation, swept back and styled.

"Just speaking from experience, Larry," I told him.

"I'll have your voucher in a couple minutes," Gracie promised, inputting the apprehension details so she could process my payment. She shot Larry a smile. "Hey there, Deputy Marshal Daniels. Looking good this morning."

Larry nodded back politely, always happy to be told how good he looked but too upset to bother with his usual flirting.

"Grant, you're wasting your talents with this bullshit. You need to move on, make a life for yourself."

I sighed, suddenly feeling very tired.

"We've had this conversation before," I reminded him. "Where the hell do you think I could get a job? You think I could get hired on anywhere in Union law enforcement the way I left?"

"The Union isn't the only one hiring out there. You could get a job in corporate security out at one of the other colonies. They'd love to have someone with your qualifications!"

I couldn't help it, this time. I laughed in his face.

"Yeah, right, that would be the perfect end for me. A disgraced former Marshal would fit right in with the corrupt head-breakers the corporates use to keep their workers in line out in the colonies. Then I could just prove to everyone including myself that Internal Affairs and Tom Caty were right about me."

I clamped my mouth shut, realizing I was getting a bit loud.

"Anyway," I went on, a bit quieter and much less strident,

"since Janie took Luke and went back to the Solar System, I got no pressing urge to settle down anywhere more permanent than a ship."

I raised a hand to forestall his next protest.

"I *do* appreciate the fact you're worried about me, Larry," I assured him. "But this way, I get to keep doing what I'm good at and get paid for it. And I kind of like the freedom. I'm sorry my being around this place embarrasses you, though. That wasn't my intention."

"Now, Grant," Larry objected, looking stricken, "you know that's not how it is…"

"Okay, Grant, here's your voucher," Gracie announced cheerfully, handing me the data crystal. "Just upload that at any terminal and you'll be good to go."

"Thanks a bunch, Gracie." I slipped the chit into my shirt pocket and was about to walk away without another word, but I figured I owed Larry better than that. "Look, this is my job now, and probably for a while. I could try working further out from the Panicle for a bit if it makes you feel better, but this is the Fugitive Recovery hub for the whole sector. I go to another sector, I don't know the lay of the land, I don't know the people, I got no connections."

Larry nodded, though I could tell from the stubborn-mule look of dissatisfaction on his face he wasn't happy with it.

"You do what you got to do, Grant," he said, then turned to walk away. "But then you always have."

The words twisted a knife in my gut. It was an old wound, a reminder my decisions had consequences for more than just me. I thought about going after him, trying to explain better, but we'd had all these conversations before and they never changed anything. My career, my marriage, my life were all ruined, and I'd dragged Larry's prospects for ever being more than a Deputy Marshal down with them. Talking more would just make it worse.

"Hey Gracie," I asked over my shoulder, still watching Larry walk away, back toward the Criminal Investigations Center where he kept an office. "Whatcha got that's hot and that'll take me out of the system for a while?"

"Not a lot hitting the wire lately," the older woman admitted, her voice wistful, as if she didn't care for the sudden influx of law and order. "I'll send it to your 'link, but the only things I saw this morning were a couple of asteroid miners who broke out of pre-trial confinement and stole an orbital transfer vehicle." She shrugged. "If they're in the rocks, with all the wildcat mining setups there, I doubt anyone'll find them."

Damn. Hopping rock to rock, homestead to homestead would take weeks, and I doubted the reward would make it worthwhile. Maybe I really *would* have to leave the system.

"Everything else is months, even years old," Gracie went on, a sympathetic lament for my prospects. "All cold case stuff no one's been able to find a lead on. It's too much to send it all, but you can use the public terminal over there." She was pointing to a data terminal set in the wall beside her station.

"Thanks, I'll give it a look."

The cases were just as cold as she'd said, all of them lacking information, clues or the promise of much return on my investment of time and resources. Except...

One caught my eye. A fugitive not from Marshals' custody but from the Navy's Military Police, oddly enough. I checked again and confirmed the fugitive was, indeed, a civilian and not military. Military personnel didn't bring as high a bounty and most hunters didn't bother with them. Her picture hovered above the details of her file. I'd become pretty good at judging people from their file picture. It caught them at a time when they were brand new to their situation, uncertain, maybe hopeful or maybe depressed but always uncertain. And then someone asked them to smile for a picture and so much about what they were feeling went into that fake smile.

Hers had been taken at the personnel section of a now-defunct company called Hadur Defense Technologies, founded back on Earth, moved to the Barnard's Star system and the industrial sections of the Paragon station there and then, finally to Epsilon Indi and the Panicle before they'd gone under. All that had been far in the future when the photo had captured the woman's hopeful smile. Her whole life and an exciting career had been ahead of her. Maybe a relationship, maybe a raise, maybe a new apartment, all those positives…and yet, her smile held just a hint of reserve, as if she knew life was never predictable, as if even then she knew anything could come along and topple it all.

She was solid-looking, neither thin nor chunky, just solid. A firm chin, high cheekbones framed broad-set eyes with keen intelligence behind their warm blue. Not what I would call pretty, but…pleasant, I guess.

I forced my eyes away from her photo and back to the details of the file. Her name was Delia Beckett, age thirty-four, and she was wanted for theft of vital military supplies and treason.

Treason, by God.

That would explain the involvement of the Navy and the MPs. It didn't say what exactly she'd stolen, but then, it wouldn't. Top secret and all that. She'd been arrested fourteen months ago, escaped two months later during a pre-trial prison transfer. Something nagged at the back of my head and I cross-checked it on my 'link.

Yeah, Hadur Defense Technologies had gone out of business only three weeks after she'd been arrested. It had been something involving her work. Not too great a leap since she worked in defense. But treason? Weren't a lot of things you could steal that would get you charged with treason, and the first one that came to mind was military-grade Bartoli crystals. They were needed for the big blaster cannons, the kind ships of the line used against each other or, and this was where the treason part came in, for planetary bombardment. No one in any level of government wanted weapons floating around that could penetrate planetary defense shields and take out whole cities, or destroy space stations. Treason was one of the very few crimes that still carried the possibility of the death penalty.

Yeah, I'd have run, too.

I looked for records of the pursuit, of any investigation, and found none. It was all heavily redacted by the Navy, but I couldn't see any indication they'd ever sent MPs after her. I frowned. It didn't make a damn bit of sense. I looked into her pre-work history, found out she'd been born on Earth, but her parents had emigrated to Morrigan, right here in Epsilon Indi, out in a region on the eastern edge of their southern hemisphere called Absolution.

Both parents dead when their hopper crashed in a sudden storm a year before Beckett had even graduated college, long before she was hired on with Hadur. Surely, the MPs had gone to Absolution, just to check on her? I mean, even the Navy had to be smart enough for that, right? Except I couldn't find anything in the records to indicate anyone had ever bothered with it. I caught myself scowling and forced a neutral expression back onto my face.

"Gracie," I said and she looked up from whatever clerical task she'd been working on behind the desk. "Could you send me the fugitive file on Delia Beckett? I'd appreciate it."

"Sure thing, sweetie," she replied automatically, then paused when she actually pulled up the file, looking at me with what might have been concern in her tiny, dark eyes. "A Navy case? Damn, Grant, there's a reason those have such a high bounty. People like that are dangerous."

"I promise to be careful," I told her, tipping an imaginary hat. "Thanks, Gracie. See you next time."

I heard the chime from my 'link telling me the file had been delivered and I weighed the little device in my hand. It seemed heavier with the data, as if it knew something I didn't. Well, I knew where I needed to go to find out what, but I didn't like it.

The Criminal Investigation Division was my old stomping ground, the place where I'd made my reputation as a Marshal… and then destroyed it. Larry worked in the Research Squad, which was a step down from our old assignment in the Fugitive Task Force, and I was the one responsible for kicking him down that step. If the dirty looks had been present on my journey through the public areas of the station, they intensified to a laser focus when I stepped into the CID section. I moved fast and purposefully, trying to avoid any questions I didn't want to answer, ducking into the doorway for Research before anyone cornered me to demand to know what I was doing there.

CID as a whole was bustling with activity, Marshals and clerks constantly on the move, either heading out to or returning from field work, cataloging evidence, recording statements. Research was the home of the unsung heroes, the people who dug up the data leading to those raids and arrests. And unsung also meant unpromoted, for the most part, and definitely unhappy. There were no smiling faces in the Research center, no high fives and no congratulatory plaques hanging on the walls. The denizens of this underworld worked silently at their stations, running one algorithm after another, digging up nuggets of data and trying to connect them together with the help of computer systems out of date before I was born.

Larry was at his desk, because of course he was, and looked to just be getting settled in for another long round of unheralded net searches, and he didn't look happy when I showed up with my "I need a favor" grin.

"No," he said immediately, shaking his head, not even looking up from the readout at his terminal.

"Larry," I said, "it's just a simple…"

"*No.*" Now he did look up, his eyes fixed in an intractable expression. "I'm already in a shithole, Grant. I'm not going to dig any deeper."

I did a quick, surreptitious check of our surroundings to make sure none of the other functionaries in the squad room were close enough to overhear. Of all the places I could wander in this station, this was the one where no one would give me a second look. You had to have hope and pride to look down on someone else, apparently.

"I'm going into a job blind," I tried to explain, speaking quickly to get the information into his head before he could interrupt. "Fugitive's name is Delia Beckett. It's a Navy MP arrest and I don't know if they bothered to follow through with an in-person visit to the last known address. Or if we…" I bit down on the word, stopping myself with a sour expression. "Or if *the Marshals* visited the place after the case was transferred here. I don't need any insider information, just if they bothered to even visit the woman's home in Absolution."

He glared at me, anger out of place on his too-handsome face, like some vandal had drawn a mustache on the Mona Lisa. Behind those eyes, though, thoughts were grinding like a milling machine.

"All right, I'll do it," he said, "*if* you make me a promise."

"Sure," I agreed readily. "Anything I can do for you, Larry."

"Go somewhere else." The words were full of such venom, I nearly took a step back.

"What, you want me to wait out in the lobby or something?"

"No!" He stopped himself and shrugged. "Well, that, *too,* yeah. But I mean, you're so free, so cut loose of all responsibility, everything that might tie you down. So, go someplace *else.* Go make a life in another system, go bug the Marshals there, and maybe they won't even know who you are and you won't get dirty looks every time you bring in a fugitive."

The vitriol faded from his voice and it became more a tone of one friend pleading with another. "Or just get out of the business, go work in a bar or use that stupid, overpriced ship of yours to run a courier service, or do *anything* that gets you out of this. Because it's going to get you killed, Grant. You're going to keep doing this shit until some moron gets the drop on you, and you're going to get killed and that's exactly what that asshole Caty wanted."

I opened my mouth to agree automatically, anything to get the information and shut him up before he lectured my ear off. But I paused instead, considering whether I was becoming exactly the sort of asshole everyone thought I was.

"All right," I promised him. "After I bring this one in, I'll move on, try another sector."

He didn't look convinced, but he waved me away.

"Go wait in the lobby."

I tried to find a shadowed corner, the furthest away from the offices, hunched down in an uncomfortable, puke-green chair next to an artificial plant. Its plastic fronds tickled at the side of my face and I wondered why they didn't bring in a real plant. It would have helped with carbon dioxide scrubbing and added some character to the place.

"Masterson, what the hell are you still doing here?" Oh, wonderful.

It was Claridge again, Francis Claridge, the blond with the buzz cut, alone now without his junior inspector sidekick to show off for. He towered over my chair, intimidating the potted plant.

"I'm wondering why you guys don't have real plants in here, truth be told."

Claridge blinked, the limited range of his imagination flummoxed by something outside its parameters, and I sat there, chin propped on my fist, waiting for his asshole implementation system to reboot.

"Seriously, Masterson," he went on when his train of thought had been levered slowly and laboriously back on the rails, "do you get off on rubbing this shit in our face? Reminding everyone here what you did?"

I regarded him through hooded eyes, trying not to take him seriously because it wouldn't do any good, but getting tired of his shtick.

"And what exactly is it you think I did, Francis?" I made the mistake of asking him. "Besides my job, that is."

He sputtered at that, the sound like one of the old-style ground-cars they use out in the boonies taking a corner too hard and nearly skidding out. Unfortunately, he was able to regain control and negotiate the curve. I'd been looking forward to him crashing and rolling.

"You abused your Goddamned authority, Masterson!" He was yelling now, loud enough to draw attention. "You pursued a case against a senior representative of the Union *after* you'd been expressly ordered to back off!"

"And I suppose the fact he's a Senior Union Rep had nothing to do with the fact I was ordered to back off, huh?" I asked, tilting my head toward him the way you might when speaking to a slow child.

"And what do you think you accomplished by illegally bugging his offices, douchebag? Do you think you're above the law? Do you think just because it's someone you think is a bad guy you get to be a bad guy, too?" Now he was bellowing and everyone was staring, even the perps being walked through in restraints.

"I didn't monitor his offices," I ground out, slowly pushing myself up from the chair. I was still shorter than Claridge, but I had a good seven or eight kilos on him and it wasn't fat. It wasn't *all* fat. "Caty had me framed to get me off his case, and if you had half the brains you do mouth, you'd know it."

"And you went and proved that by assaulting him?" he bellowed back at me. "By getting yourself arrested and hauled off in cuffs in front of everyone like a fucking criminal? You made us *all* look bad! You're making us look bad just by being here! You're a fucking disgrace to the Union Marshal Service and just looking at you makes me sick!"

That about did it. I'm phlegmatic by nature, or at least I like to think I am, but there's a point where my heels go back against the wall. I knew all the signs; I'd been there before. Everything seemed to slip into slow motion, and my focus narrowed into an auditory and visual tunnel aimed at Francis Claridge. I analyzed his stance, ran through what I remembered of his unarmed combat training sessions and had decided on a plan of attack in the space of about a half a second, and we were about to find out which one of us had paid more attention in that training when a clear, commanding voice cut through the haze of adrenaline.

"What in the living hell is going on out here?"

The woman was tiny, at least a head shorter than me and maybe fifty kilos soaking wet, a child playing dress-up in her blue Marshal's coveralls, but both Claridge and I locked up immediately, coming to attention. For me, it was old instinct and respect, since I wasn't under her command anymore.

"Senior Inspector," Claridge stuttered, "I'm sorry, there was just a disagreement…"

"Yes, Deputy Marshal Claridge," she cut him off, her voice the crack of a whip. "I *heard* the disagreement. Everyone in the damned *station* heard it. I'd be surprised if there aren't ships a million klicks away that heard your disagreement!"

"Yes, ma'am," Claridge said meekly. "I'm sorry, ma'am."

"You are a Union Marshal, Claridge. You deal with criminals, murderers, the scum of the galaxy every single day. You are supposed to be professional and calm in the face of all this. It's your *job*. Do you understand me?"

"Yes, ma'am," he said. "No excuse, ma'am."

"You're not a freaking Academy cadet, Claridge. Don't give me that 'no excuse' bullshit. Just go cool off and don't let me hear this sort of shit from you again." He began to splutter acknowledgement but she waved him away like she was chasing off a mosquito. "Just go!"

He shot me a dirty look before he hurried away, leaving me alone with Maggie Tanaka. She'd been the scourge of the sector for fifteen years and a personal hero of mine, once. Now, I felt as if I were her greatest disappointment and if I'm being honest, I'd come to hate her.

"What do you want from this place, Grant?" she asked, exasperation in her tone but no real anger. Probably she was beyond anger and into "don't-give-a-shit" territory.

"I came to drop off a bounty and search for the next one, ma'am." I held up my 'link. "I sat down for a minute to read the file on the new fugitive and Francis started running his mouth."

Tanaka sighed.

"As a licensed bounty hunter, you are allowed by law to operate out of any Marshal's station in the Union," she said as if she were reading the words out of a manual. "And the lobby is accessible by the public, so you are within your rights to sit here as long as you do not make yourself a public nuisance. But I don't need my people distracted, Masterson, so if you *are* going to be here, you need to swallow your damn pride and keep your mouth shut no matter what a hothead like Claridge does. Otherwise, I'll have you declared persona non grata and kicked out of here permanently."

"Understood, ma'am."

She seemed to be waiting for something more, but that was all I was going to give her.

"Jesus, Grant," she sighed, fists planted on her hips. "I know you're a stubborn son of a bitch, but can't you just move on?"

This time she didn't wait for an answer, just stalked back to her office, leaving me alone and embarrassed. I didn't like being embarrassed. It brought up a side of me I tried not to indulge, the side that liked to hurt people. I'd given into that urge when I visited Tomas Caty the day after I'd found out about his attempt to frame me for bugging his office. It had felt pretty damn satisfying, feeling his nose crunch under my knuckles, seeing the blood spray off of his face.

But his nose looked just fine now, after a visit to one of the high-end clinics available to Union Reps, and my career was over. I could have just seen through the investigation, let it play out. There was enough reasonable doubt that I probably just would have had a black mark on my record, maybe a hold on promotion for a few years, but I'd still have been a Marshal. Instead, I'd given him exactly what he wanted.

"Jesus, I can't leave you alone for two minutes," Larry said, disgust heavy in his voice. I'd been so busy feeling sorry for myself, I hadn't even heard him walk up behind me.

"Yeah," I agreed. "I'm just a mess."

"Remember our bargain." He raised a warning finger. "I tell you this, you have to leave the sector."

"I remember."

"Well, the answer to your question is no." For a second, I thought he was saying he wasn't going to help, but he went on. "No one ever visited Absolution looking for this Delia Beckett. Not us, not the MPs."

"Don't you find that strange?" I asked him, more to bounce my thoughts off of someone than out of any interest in his answer. "Lady's wanted for treason, a death sentence crime, and the MPs never even bothered to visit the planet she last lived on before she left for school."

"File says her parents are dead and she has no living relatives on Morrigan," he said, his shrug expressively disinterested. "Maybe they just figured a wanted fugitive wouldn't be stupid enough to just head straight back home."

I spared him a baleful glance.

"If I've learned anything working this job, Larry," I told him, "it's that desperate people *always* go home." I took a last, long look around the station before I headed for the exit. "It's all they've got left."

[3]

I LET Dog land the *Charietto*. I told him it was because I was tired, and I was. I hadn't slept well the night before we pulled out of the Panicle. I think too much of what Larry and Inspector Tanaka had said were bouncing around inside my head.

But the truth was, Dog is a better pilot than I am, which might have something to do with the way he can hook right into the ship's computer and might also have something to do with the fact all my Marshal's training was in investigative procedures, hand to hand combat and firearms proficiency. I had a single semester at the Academy on flying a starship and it had boiled down to: "let the computer fly it, you're not a damned pilot."

I was *trying* to get better at it. The *Charietto* was my home now and I felt like I should be able to handle her better, but it was a work in progress and that morning I didn't feel like getting a strained neck bouncing the landing gear off the spaceport pavement.

"Independent Transport *Charietto*, you are down," the helpful, automated voice of spaceport traffic control informed us, as if we might have thought we were still in the air despite the jolt of hitting the ground and all. "You will be assessed port fees for a minimum of one local day at the normal rates. Further charges will be accrued at ten-hour intervals. Please have a nice stay on Morrigan."

"I hate chatty computers," Dog told me, shaking his muzzle. "You want me to hire us a flyer?"

"That'd attract too much attention," I said, shaking my head. I hit the quick-release for my seat harness and pulled the latch to pivot the pilot's acceleration couch around, pushing up and climbing out of the cockpit back to the utility bay. "We'll rent a groundcar."

"That'll take forever," Dog complained, hopping down after me with an agility I envied.

"What do you care?" I asked him, pulling my gunbelt out of the equipment locker and strapping it on. "You worried about wasting time? You're a machine, you could conceivably live forever."

"You know they base Artificial Intelligence systems on human brains, right, genius?" Dog tilted his head at me, one ear drooping. "That means I think like a human, and time passes at the same rate for me as it does for you."

"And yet somehow, you're so much less patient than me," I muttered, grabbing my hat. It was felt, hand-made, modeled after an old Earth fashion called a Stetson. My ex-wife had bought it for me as a joke, and I'd never had the nerve to wear it when I was actually a Marshal, but one of the advantages of self-employment is enforcing your own dress code. Stetsons were required for all humans working at Grant Masterson Fugitive Recovery, Inc.

I hit the control to open the side hatch, then kicked the pedal to extend the boarding ladder. It was mid-day in the high plains of Philyra and a hot wind blew dust into my face through the open hatch, forcing me to pull my hat down over my eyes.

"Dang," I commented, pulling out a pair of protective goggles and slipping them on before replacing my hat and trying again.

"I'm beginning to agree with the MPs," Dog said, standing in the open hatchway and staring out at the glare of Epsilon Indi. "Why the hell would anyone come back *here*?"

Philyra wasn't much. It wasn't the largest city on Morrigan, but it was close enough they'd given it a spaceport. If you wanted to call this a spaceport. It was a paved landing field, though I could barely make out the pavements through the drifts of dust and sand turning everything yellow, including the air. There was a traffic control building out in the middle of it all, surrounded by radar and lidar equipment, and the whole place was ringed by a high fence. There was only one way out, and that went right through the customs' facility. I'd seen from the air that the transportation rental offices were just beyond customs, and I'd been hoping for a spot near the exit. Instead, it was going to be a long walk.

The *Charietto* hurt to look at in the mid-day light, the polished silver of her delta-winged hull gleaming in reflected brilliance. It wasn't a stylistic choice, just a practical one—it was hard to get rid of waste heat in space, so it was vital to reflect back as much of it as possible. She was about as small as a starship could get and still be useful, little more to her than engines, a cockpit, two small cabins and a utility area that could be used at need as a galley, a workshop, or a medical clinic. When I'd first bought the ship, I'd worried I would go crazy cooped up with so little room, but there was something homey about her now.

And of course, after a couple weeks, I got used to the smell. I scrubbed and scrubbed, but it's really hard to get rid of the stench of fugitives who don't particularly like being locked in the spare cabin and show their displeasure by not taking advantage of the chemical toilet in the ship's head. Dog is lucky, he can shut off his senses when he wants to. I'd thought about leaving the hatch open and airing the ship out while we were planetside, but I would've wound up with three or four centimeters of dust on the deck when I got back.

Morrigan, like most colony worlds, may be habitable, but isn't really a pleasant place to live. Not like Earth. Even with what we've done to the planet, it's where we humans evolved. We were made for it, we can live on every continent. Other worlds, there are parts where we can scratch out a living, but most of the planet isn't livable for humans.

Morrigan is just slightly hotter on average than Earth, and just slightly dryer, but what "just slightly" means on a planetary scale is, most of the world is too hot and too dry for humans to survive without special protection. The areas just south and north of the poles are the nicest. Philyra was slightly outside that zone, well into "this sucks" territory, and Absolution was officially in the "this really sucks, why do we live here again?" zone. There was talk about terraforming the planet, making everything cooler and wetter, but most of those plans involved evacuating the world for a few decades and hitting it with water ice asteroids and the people who lived there tended to be against it.

"How come fugitives never hide anyplace nice?" I asked Dog plaintively, falling into a quick walk toward the customs' station. "Like tropical islands or ski resorts with lots of hot springs?"

"Who would bother to pay you to chase crooks down in some tropical paradise?" Dog was always the logical one.

"Okay, time to get all woof-woof," I reminded him. We were coming up on the customs building and other travelers were walking or driving in from their shuttles and spaceships, funneled in toward the gate by the narrowing pavement. "You dumb dog, me cheap human."

He barked and somehow managed to make it sound sarcastic. It's a real talent.

"Name and purpose for your visit?"

The customs agent seemed just as bored as a man might get

sitting at the same desk all day watching one person after another pass through, asking them the same questions and knowing their lives were infinitely more interesting than his own. He barely even eyed my gun.

"Grant Masterson, licensed bounty hunter." I handed him my credentials before he asked and his eyes opened a bit wider. Apparently, they didn't get bounty hunters very often.

"Everything is in order," he confirmed after checking my license against his database. Then he caught sight of Dog and frowned. "You do know there's a thirty-day quarantine on all animals imported from off-planet…," he began.

"He's a robot." It was an old song-and-dance I went through every time.

The customs agent glanced at me sidelong, skeptical, but ran a quick scan with his hand-held sensor wand and nodded in obvious surprise.

"He's a damned lifelike one," he said and it felt like a compliment.

"Woof," Dog commented.

The agent frowned at him, far too thoughtful for my comfort.

"I need to get him looked at," I said, shaking my head. "That bark is improperly calibrated."

"Yeah, well, you're good to go."

"Where's the local law enforcement offices?" I asked. "I need to consult with your constable or sheriff or whatever you guys have around here."

"The Philyra police station is in town." He waved back behind us, out the exit. "There's only one road into town and the station is on it about a kilometer after you hit the city limits."

"You sure you want to do that?" Dog asked me once we'd walked out the exit and were alone again with the howl of the wind to cover our voices from passers-by. "Remember what happened the last time you consulted with the locals? Shit, these small-town cops don't even like the Marshals, much less bounty hunters. They're like as not to go warn this Beckett woman you're coming."

"It's a legal requirement," I argued, but only weakly. He was right. "Well, it's a legal requirement I inform them I'm here. I don't think it specifies at exactly what point in my visit I have to notify them."

"I'm just a dog, pal, but I'd say the best time to talk to the local cops is shortly after you have Beckett in handcuffs."

I slowed in my pace, looking back and forth between the car rental office straight ahead and the single, two-lane, dusty road into town.

"Let's go get a vehicle," I said. "I'll decide when I get behind the wheel."

———

If Philyra had been not much, Absolution was even less. There were a few squared-off, pre-fab corrugated-aluminum industrial buildings, identical down to the pitting from wind-blown sand and the faded yellow paint job they shared. None bothered with a sign or advertising, but I guessed they were the fabrication center and storehouses for raw materials, pretty much universal in any town on any colony I'd ever visited. Various other shops and stores and eateries were huddled around and among them, like children hiding behind their parents' legs.

The only traffic we'd seen on the road out here had been a couple of ancient, creaking cargo trucks, rocking back and forth rhythmically with the ruts in the track, their beds loaded down with the finished product of whatever the hell they made out here. I hadn't bothered to look it up, though I had to assume it involved dust somehow because that seemed to be what they had most of.

"You made the right decision skipping the police station,"

Dog assured me as I shifted our rental into park in front of what advertised itself as a General Store. It looked pretty general, and also looked like it was a miracle it was still in business, because no one was around.

"Of course, you think it was the right decision. It was your idea."

The door of the old, beat-up rover stuck and I had to slam my shoulder into it to get it open. I waited, gesturing for Dog to follow me, but he shot me a disdainful look and tilted his head toward the door on his side. I sighed and slammed my door. I thought hard about leaving him in the vehicle, but the last time I'd tried that, he'd started whimpering and putting on the "I'm a dog stuck in a hot car" act and someone had busted out the window. I hadn't got my deposit back on that one.

I yanked open the passenger door and he hopped out, tail wagging.

"Bitch," I murmured, slamming the door shut.

"Cur, if you want to get technical."

The clerk behind the counter of the store looked up at our entry and his eyebrows kept on raising when he saw it was a stranger, went up even further when he saw Dog.

"We don't allow…," he began.

"He's a robot."

"Woof."

"That's…" He trailed off, staring at Dog with a quizzical expression on his long, horsey face.

"I'm looking for a woman named Delia Beckett. Her family lived around here until ten years ago or so and I thought she might have come back this way." I shoved my 'link at him, her file photo displayed. I didn't give him time to ask questions, barely gave him time to absorb what I was asking. It was a technique. You didn't want to give them the opportunity to come up with a plausible lie. "You know her? You seen her lately?"

"I, uh…" he dithered and I could tell almost immediately he was going to deny it and he was lying. "I've never heard of…"

"Okay, thanks," I cut him off, slipping the 'link back in my jacket pocket. "Where's the best place to get a bite to eat around here?" I grinned. "Just kidding." There was only one restaurant, unless I wanted to grab a burger and a mouthful of dust while I stood at a wooden rail.

"Why you interested in that woman?" he finally had the presence of mind to ask. "Whoever she might be," he added with affected casualness.

"She's wanted for treason, theft of vital military property and escaping federal custody. There's a fairly sizable government reward for her capture." I tipped my hat to him. "I'm Grant Masterson, licensed bounty hunter, and I'd be willing to give a portion of that reward to whoever provided information leading to her apprehension." I twirled a finger around in the air, indicating the general vicinity. "I'll be around in case you think of anything."

He was still gabbling when we went out the door. I stood on the steps as it closed behind us, regarding the other buildings of the town carefully.

"You were all impressive and tough and everything," Dog allowed, "but we still don't know anything."

"Sure, we do. We know she's here and we know they know she's here. All we have to do now is find someone willing to tell us where she's staying."

"We know all that?" It's hard for a robot Dog to look skeptical, but somehow, he managed it.

"Let's go get some lunch," I suggested. "I hear the restaurant here's strictly five star."

I might have been exaggerating, but Greta's Grill did have a great cheeseburger.

There were only five people in the whole place today,

including the cook, the dishwasher and the waitress. They were all real humans instead of touch screens because out here, it was cheaper to pay someone to work for you than to repair machinery. Spare parts were expensive, fabricator time was expensive and trained technicians were in high demand and not likely to waste their time repairing order kiosks at a diner.

"We don't allow dogs…" the waitress had greeted me on the way through the door.

"He's a robot."

"Are you sure?" She'd seemed skeptical, hands on her hips, eyebrow arched.

I'd stopped, pushing the door shut against a wind determined to fill the place with dust.

"Well, either he's a robot or someone's been feeding him and cleaning up his poop behind my back for the last year." I'd frowned. "In which case, I'd have to start charging that person rent."

That had seemed to convince her, or maybe it had convinced her I was armed and unbalanced and she shouldn't antagonize me. Either way, the cheeseburger was pretty damn good. Real cows out here, not processed soy like most people got, or even vat-grown meat like the rich folks ate to make themselves feel enlightened. The fries, however, were soggy, and I was disappointed in the lack of attention to proper French fry procedure.

"Why you heeled, cowboy?" the waitress asked me when she brought me a refill of my water. She was staring at my holstered blaster. "You think this shithole is full of desperados?"

She was cute, especially for a place like this, and could get away with being snarky.

"I am a licensed bounty hunter," I told her. "And while I don't usually need a gun to bring in fugitives, it is part of the tools of the trade and I figure I may as well take advantage of all of them."

She shaped a silent whistle, now seeming even more intrigued.

"Bounty hunter, huh? We don't get any of those in Absolution, not since I've been alive. You looking for an escaped criminal out here?" She snorted. "Hell, if I was a criminal, I'd go someplace nice."

Dog nudged me.

"Yeah, I know," I said to him quietly.

"I can assume then," I told her, "that you don't know of any fugitives in the area? Maybe a woman in her thirties, looks something like this? There's a cut of the reward in it for you if you have."

I held up the 'link so she could see the picture. She was better than the clerk at the store. He'd practically taken out an ad to let me know he was lying, but she just had the slightest of tells, a tightening around her eyes and a shifting of her jaw.

"Can't say as I've ever seen her, mister."

"Oh, well." I shrugged. "Couldn't hurt to ask. You guys got any dessert?"

The apple pie was decent, though I didn't know where the hell they got the apples from. Probably imported them from close to the poles because the pie cost an arm and a leg.

"Is this your idea of an investigation?" Dog asked me *sotto voce* when the waitress was in the back and none of the other three customers were paying attention. "At this rate, you're gonna eat us out of a reward."

"You saw the town as well as I did," I told him.

"Better. I saw it in infrared and thermal, too."

"Okay, then. If she lives in this town, she's going to show up either here or at the bar next store. If not today, then tomorrow."

"Not if everyone you've been mouthing off to tells her to stay away because there's a bounty hunter in town," Dog pointed out.

"That's a risk," I agreed. "But this is a small town. If anyone here's got a beef with her, or just needs money, they're going to hear about the reward and want a piece of it."

Dog sighed, which is an odd sound to be coming from something that doesn't breathe.

"I guess not every bounty is going to be naked robot hookers and gunfights."

"Well, I hope not. A man needs a break every now and again."

I hadn't been in the restaurant for half an hour but I guess, as I had told Dog, that news travelled fast in a little town like this. The door pushed open with a warm gust of wind and I looked up.

Local law enforcement on colony worlds can wear a variety of different uniforms, from camouflage military-style fatigues, to a traditional blue, to nothing but a jacket with their seal sewn into it, but you can always tell them. There's a certain air to them, slightly harried, as if they have too much responsibility and not enough people to handle it, and yet also a sense of absolute power, like being out on the ass-end of nowhere means there's no one to second-guess them. It's a strange and sometimes dangerous combination.

This particular example was dressed somewhere in the middle between civilian clothes and a traditional uniform, the jeans and boots not particularly saying "law enforcement," but the brown jacket and dress shirt bearing the markings of the Absolution District Constabulary, which I thought was a bit grandiose for something that probably had three employees at the very most. The pistol at her hip was not grandiose at all. It seemed worn and used and right at home. Her hand rested on it, ready to pull, and I got the feeling I was the reason.

"Good afternoon, officer," I said, nodding toward her. I would have tipped my hat, but I didn't wear it indoors. It wasn't polite. I didn't get up because she was already nervous enough and I didn't want her to think I was about to pull on her.

"Are you the bounty hunter I been told about?" she asked, not returning the pleasantries. I let it go, but it was disappointing. There's always time to be polite.

I fished my bonafides out of my jacket pocket and passed them to her slowly and carefully. She took it between thumb and forefinger, holding it away from her like it was radioactive.

"Grant Masterson, licensed by the Union Fugitive Recovery Department," I added, keeping my hand away from my gun.

The woman studied the document for several moments, much longer than she needed to, as if she expected it to suddenly give up some new secret not originally printed on it, then she tossed it back to me with a negligent snap of her wrist. I caught it in mid-air, not wanting to look like a dumbass rube and let it hit my chest, which was what she had in mind. I think she looked disappointed.

"You're supposed to consult with local law enforcement," she reminded me, "whenever you're searching for a fugitive."

"I fully intended to," I assured her. I gestured at the remains of the burger on my plate. "I was just grabbing a bite to eat first." I winked. "They got great cheeseburgers here, you know?"

She scowled at my attempt at humor, for which I couldn't blame her. I've never been that good at it. It was only then that she seemed to notice Dog, which I also couldn't blame her for, since she'd been more focused on my blaster and the possible threat it presented. Dog was half under the table and when he saw her eyes on him, he wagged his tail hopefully.

"This is a restaurant…" she began and I rubbed tiredly at my temples.

"He's a robot."

She scowled again. It seemed to be her default expression and I wondered if she was a robot, too, and needed a factory reset.

"You're here looking for someone." It wasn't a question, but I answered it anyway.

"This woman." I held up my 'link with Beckett's picture and

added the spiel about her crimes and the reward. Deputy Grouchyface might not be interested, but there were other customers. "Any chance she's sitting in your jail cell on a drunken disorderly and I can go home early?"

"I've never seen her. Maybe you got the wrong town, Mr. Masterson."

"I might," I agreed. "But I got the rental car for the rest of today, so I might as well keep looking."

She grunted noncommittally.

"Don't cause any trouble. And notify me if you make an apprehension."

"Of course, officer."

"Constable," she corrected me. "Constable Edlund."

"It was a pleasure meeting you, Constable Edlund."

She turned and headed back out the door, still watching me over her shoulder.

A few of the other patrons who'd drifted in while I'd been eating stared at her, and at me. I paid the bill and pushed up from the table.

"Come on," I urged Dog. "Let's go see if that bar's open."

"Who's gonna be at a bar *this* early?" he asked me after we'd passed through the door and back out into a steady wind that could mask his voice from the few dusty, vacant-eyed locals walking by.

"Drunks, I hope."

$$[\ 4\ ]$$

I WAS NOT DISAPPOINTED. If there's one thing you can count on in a Podunk, nowhere town on a Podunk, nowhere colony, it's afternoon drunks. Not just workers having a beer at the end of their shift, I'm talking about the losers who've lost their last three jobs and hate their life and are intent on spending every credit they can scrounge pouring liquid comfort down their throats because it's better than sitting around sober realizing what utter pieces of crap they are.

Not that I have any experience with this myself.

This was the perfect bar to find people like that, dim and dingy and beaten down by the environment. The walls were cracked, the floor perpetually covered in dust, the windows small and braced by shutters to keep out the ever-present wind. There were tables, but they were unoccupied. Tables were for parties, for friends, for groups. The people I was looking for would be alone, sitting at the bar, waiting for life to come to them.

I went to them.

There were three at the moment, two men and a woman, evenly spaced around the bar, trying not to get too close to each other, afraid too much of the stench of failure would build up and cause an explosion. I chose one of the men. I'd tried to pry information from a drunk woman too many times and it usually ended with them thinking, for good or ill, that I was coming onto them. Sometimes that helped to loosen them up, but extricating myself was always much more complicated.

I sat down beside a man who could have been anywhere between forty and a hundred and forty, depending on how much money he'd started out with before he'd wound up here. His hair was shot with grey through tight curls of brown, his face cracked and lined, weathered by time and exposure to sun and wind. His clothes were plain, not ragged or torn but work clothes just the same. Old grease stains darkened the sleeves, long faded, showing the duration of his current unemployment.

He didn't look up at me when I sat down, but his perpetual frown deepened.

"There must be a lot of other places you could sit," he murmured. Then he did look over, eyes widening. "Did you bring a fucking dog into the bar? How did they let you get away with that?"

I sighed. That was getting old.

"You want another drink?" I asked him, nodding at his nearly empty glass of something clear and cheap and alcoholic.

"I ain't your type, cowboy," he grunted in dark amusement.

"Are you the type who'd like to make a few easy credits just for telling me what you know?"

"I don't know shit." He downed the dregs of the drink, his words and body language sounding final…but he didn't get up, didn't leave the bar.

"Tell you what," I offered, fishing a few strips of paper money out of my pocket, "I'll buy you a drink. In exchange, you listen to what I need to know. If you can give me something useful, there's a lot more in it for you."

"Fine." He grabbed the bills and waved them at the bartender, who seemed just as old and embittered as the drunk, if more economically secure. "Another vodka, Grimaldi."

The bartender took the money but eyed the man skeptically. "I'll get you another drink, Cappy, but you throw up again," Grimaldi warned him, "and you'll have to buy your booze in a bag and drink outside."

"It was just the one time," Cappy insisted, but the bartender had already turned away.

"Her," I told Cappy, holding the picture up for him. "I want to know about her."

His eyes narrowed as if he couldn't quite see straight and needed to concentrate to actually focus on the image. He knew her. I don't know if he'd ever been good at concealing his emotions, but years of alcoholism hadn't done him any favors when it came to controlling his face.

"Why you interested in her?"

"She's a fugitive, I'm a bounty hunter. There's a reward. You help me, you get ten percent of it."

"Fifty," he said with mulish stubbornness.

"Ten."

"Forty-five."

"Ten." I eyed him balefully. "I got expenses to make and a ship to pay off. Time, I got plenty of. I can stay here for a week sleeping in my ship, paying next to nothing, coming back every day."

I didn't mention the car rental, which would begin to build up over a week. He didn't need to know.

"I want it up front," Cappy said. "I ain't waiting till you haul her back to the Marshals."

"Fine," I said, raising my hands palms-up. "You get it when I get her. Where is she?"

He checked around him, as if he expected someone to be listening. The bartender was still pouring his drink and Cappy waited until he'd set it down in front of him and walked away before he continued.

"She's calling herself Rebecca Mitchell," he whispered, leaning close enough I could smell the vodka on his breath, could tell he hadn't had a shower in a few days. I forbore since I really did need the information. "I don't know where she lives, but she works driving a feed truck out to the cattle ranches." He chortled, as if it was the biggest joke in the world. "Bitch comes in here every night after her shift for three or four beers, but she thinks she's too good for me, like it's some horrible thing I get here a couple hours before she does."

"What time does her shift end?" I asked, not bothering to give him my opinion on Ms. Mitchell *nee* Beckett's selectivity toward men.

Cappy squinted at the data board above the bar, where the time, temperature, weather forecast and latest news got replayed every few minutes.

"Two hours," he told me. "Now, where's my money."

"After I have her in cuffs and in my car," I reminded him.

"What, don't you trust me?" He seemed truly aggrieved.

"If I were ever of a mind to start trusting people," I advised him, sliding off the bar stool and heading for the door, "I very much doubt I'd start here."

———

I waited in my rental. Sitting in a bar full of hopeless dead-enders didn't seem like a productive use of my time, nor did it seem like a good way to stay out of sight and leave the coast clear for Delia Beckett. Dog wasn't happy about it, though.

"It's boring out here," he insisted for perhaps the third time in —I checked the clock—the last two hours and twenty minutes. "Didn't the old drunk say she'd be here by now?"

"He did," I admitted. I leaned down further in the seat and watched the stars beginning to come out over the eastern horizon. At night, the town turned rather picturesque, I thought. "But he's a drunk. He might not have the times exactly right." I shrugged. "He might not have her workdays right. Or he might have been lying."

"You know, Masterson," Dog said, resting his chin on the center console and regarding me with what I thought of as his philosophical look, "humans are mortal."

"Yes, I was aware of that."

"You have some of the nanites left in your blood from the Marshals Service Induction Medical, I know that. I can sense them. They'll keep you young and healthy for longer than normal, but eventually, you'll die."

"I was aware of that, too." I tipped my hat down over my eyes. "You coming to a point or are these lines strictly parallel?"

"You only have so many years in your life. Why are you wasting them sitting in a fucking rental car in the parking lot of a bar in a colony cow town?"

"Oh, good God," I moaned. "Who the hell have you been talking to, my ex-wife?"

"Hey, it's all the same to me, pal," Dog pointed out. "I'm going to live forever as long as some idiot doesn't let me get damaged so badly, I can't be repaired. I don't have a biological imperative to reproduce, which means I have no need to succeed at something in order to be important enough for someone to want to mate with me. I'm good just sitting here, observing, collecting data, fetching the occasional tennis ball."

I shot him a curious look.

"You actually like doing that?"

"A dog has his programming. Besides, it can be fun, as long as the human doesn't throw like an infant." He glared at me.

"I swear I will do better. Throwing the tennis ball, I mean. I'm not changing jobs."

Dog might or might not have been prepared to keep arguing, but he never got the chance. I recognized the grumbling engine of a large cargo truck, internal combustion like you often see out in the less developed colonies. Lot easier to fabricate parts for a cylinder-driven engine than to find the precious metals and chemicals necessary for a battery-run vehicle...unless you've got enough money to power your truck on Bartoli crystals, and no one out here would bother. Not when you can distill alcohol and build an engine in a workshop for next to nothing.

That's the thing about colonies they don't tell you in the corporate recruiting videos they stream in school. They have to run a profit, and with the costs of transporting people and cargo and amortizing the huge initial investment, the corners that get cut are luxuries. Colonists raising cattle or mining bauxite or whatever don't *need* virtual reality entertainment or luxury flyers or the latest in expensive fabricator patterns or smart houses. They can get by just fine on old, beater trucks and local materials for their buildings and home-brewed whiskey.

I even recognized the pattern the flatbed truck had been built from. It was something from about 500 years ago, all the way from pre-starflight Earth, with the old, boxy lines and huge windshield, a design from a company called China Star. It was a bear to drive and I'd have been hating life if I had to haul feed back and forth in one over these roads every day. Which, I suppose, was why the job was available and no one asked any questions when the applicant didn't provide any identification or references.

Delia Beckett looked a bit rougher around the edges than she had in her file photo from Hadur Defense, but a year on the run might do that to a person. Her firm solidity had wasted away to a gaunt look, as if her skin was stretched out over her skull, and her stylishly coifed corporate hair was stringy and pulled back into a simple ponytail. She hadn't changed her looks, hadn't tried to have cosmetic surgery. Maybe she didn't have the money for it, or maybe she just wasn't savvy enough to realize it might have helped.

Her skin looked white and washed out through the windshield of the truck. She'd pulled it into the space right across from me, like she'd known I was there and had come to surrender. She shifted the truck into park, fatigue dragging at her shoulders, then sat back and rested her head against the back of her seat for nearly thirty seconds before she finally climbed out, slowly and without enthusiasm.

"This is too darn easy," I muttered, pushing my door open, adjusting my hat to give me a better line of sight.

"You're always complaining," Dog said, hopping out through my door instead of waiting for me to open his. "Let's go make some money."

"I'll do the talking,"

I was ready to run to cut her off before she reached the front door of the bar, but she was shuffling, seemingly in no hurry to get there or anywhere else. I stepped between two work trucks and directly into her path, with Dog circling around to back me up.

"Delia Beckett," I said, hand resting on the butt of my gun, "you're a fugitive from the Union Marshal's Service and as a duly licensed independent agent of the Fugitive Recovery Division, I am placing you under arrest."

I wasn't sure what I expected from Delia. She'd been on the run a long time and she was obviously tired, either from her life or of it, but on the other hand, she was wanted for a death-sentence offense and you never know how someone will react with mortality staring them in the face. I've had the meekest looking, mousy little people come at me like a caged tiger…

Delia sighed and her shoulders rolled as if a weight were

shifting off of them. I could have sworn I saw pale brown dust puffing off her grey work coveralls from the move, as if she'd become part of the earth-tone landscape.

"I guess I've been expecting this," she admitted, not moving a step either to run or attack. "I'm kind of surprised it took this long." Her voice was rough and raspy, like she'd been smoking twenty cigarettes a day for the last year, or it might have been from breathing in the dust. Her eyes wouldn't look up, wouldn't meet mine. "It's been so long, I'd convinced myself they didn't really want to catch me."

I pulled a pair of flex cuffs out of my jacket pocket and stepped around her, holding them up so she could see what I was doing.

"I've found the federal government to be fairly persistent when it comes to treason," I said, gently but firmly pulling her hands behind her back and fastening the restraints. She smelled of dust and hay and work. Not an unpleasant scent, sort of homey. "I doubt they'd give up quite that easy."

"It's so much more complicated than that," she said, her face finally raising to meet my eyes as if she wanted to tell me something vital. But then she shrugged. "It doesn't matter. It's safer for you if you don't know."

That seemed like an odd thing for her to say. I'd arrested a lot of fugitives, both as a Marshal and a bounty hunter, and if there was one thing every single one had in common, it was an almost compulsive need to explain to me how they were really innocent, how it wasn't fair and they were being framed. Not one had ever suggested they didn't want me to know what had happened.

"Is there anything you need from your truck before we go?" I asked, pulling her gently but steadily back toward my rental. "Anyone you want to leave a message for?"

She laughed softly, and bitterness hardened the brittle edges of her face.

"I've lived here a year and I don't think there's anyone I've met who would realize I was gone except the feed company. Their truck has a transponder. They'll know where to find it."

Now that sort of reaction I was more used to. I walked her to the passenger door of my car, Dog circling wide, patrolling the parking lot for threats. When he barked, my head snapped around and my blaster came halfway out of its holster before I saw who was approaching from the other side of the lot, across the street from the restaurant.

"Lovely evening, Constable Edlund," I said, letting my blaster slide back into place. Her pistol was in her hand, held at low ready as she stepped toward me, squared off. "Anything I can do for you?"

"I thought I told you to consult with me before you made an apprehension, bounty hunter." Her voice was flat, unamused, unhappy.

"I happened upon Ms. Beckett while I was here for a drink," I explained. "I was going to head right over to your office and inform you immediately, I swear."

Yeah, it was a pretty transparent lie, but it covered my ass and she couldn't prove I was lying. I don't like dealing with colonial law enforcement. All too often, they get the job because no one else wants it, and keep it because they wind up in someone's pocket. Even the honest ones don't give a damn about a federal warrant and especially aren't keen on the idea of lining a bounty hunter's pockets. So yeah, I might bend the requirements sometimes about keeping them informed.

"You're not taking this woman anywhere, Masterson," Edlund declared. "I have nothing but your word she's even the same person in your warrant and your word don't mean *shit* to me." She raised her handgun, the muzzle level with my chest, and nodded sharply at Beckett. "Set Ms. Mitchell free, then turn around and put your hands on the car."

Ms. Mitchell. So, she'd known exactly who Beckett was, and who she was pretending to be. But according to Beckett, she had no friends here to contact, so Edlund wasn't doing this for personal reasons.

Dog growled low in his throat from somewhere off to my right and Edlund's muzzle swept briefly in that direction, her eyes widening.

"Call off your dog, Masterson," she snapped at me.

"What's that hogleg you're carrying, Constable?" I asked her, my tone casual, friendly, as if she weren't trying to arrest me. "Not a blaster, not out on Morrigan. Not with the budget of a cow town constabulary. Is it an old-time slug shooter? Gunpowder maybe, with metal bullets, maybe even brass cartridge casings way out here?"

"It's enough to put a damned hole in you if you don't call off your dog, Masterson." She tried to sound intimidating, but it was coming across scared.

"He's not a dog, Constable Edlund," I reminded her. "He's a robot. Night vision. Sonar. Runs about fifty kilometers an hour and got really wicket metal teeth. More like a shark's than a real dog." Okay, that part was a lie. "And your slug shooter, even if it's a big-ass slug, 10mm, 12mm…well, unless you get really lucky here in the dark, it's just gonna bounce right off his endoskeleton, you know?"

Another growl, much further away than the first one, and on the other side of the constable. Her jaw clenched, teeth bared to the night, reflecting the light from the bar's windows.

"Constable Edlund," Delia Beckett said, loud and clear, cutting through the hiss of the wind. "I am Delia Beckett and I am a wanted fugitive. Wanted for treason and theft of sensitive military goods. I am the woman he's looking for. Please don't put yourself at risk for me." Her voice became small. "I'm not worth it."

I squinted back at the woman, even more confused now. I'd never had a prisoner talk like that. I shook the thoughts away. More immediate business.

If looks could kill, I'd have been dead on the ground from Edlund's glare, but she holstered her weapon.

"Get your ass out of my town this second, Masterson. I don't want to see you in this place again. I don't care what it is, I'll find a reason to stick you in a holding cell until even your own mother forgets what you look like."

I nodded, opening the back door of the car and guiding Beckett into the rear seat, fastening the restraints across her. With her hands cuffed in back, she couldn't release them. Then I opened the front door.

"Dog."

I didn't have to yell. I hadn't been lying about his hearing. Or his speed. He shot out of the night like a bullet, just a blur until he jumped into the seat and grinned open-mouthed back at Edlund, exposing my exaggeration about his teeth. I shut the door and he was still grinning through the window, his eyes focused on the Constable, just in case.

I didn't look back at her, just climbed behind the wheel and began backing out of the space.

"Thanks for speaking up," I told Beckett. "That could have been awkward for everyone."

"No one else needs to get hurt because of me," she said, eyes fixed on the back of the seat in front of her, voice dull and lifeless. "I should have just let them kill me."

"That's between you and a Union military court," I said, pulling out onto the road. "I'm just doing a job."

No response, but I hadn't expected one. Dog cocked an eye at me, curious, whining slightly and giving me one of those looks that said he thought something smelled wrong. Metaphorically.

"Shut up," I told him. "I'm driving here."

[5]

BECKETT DIDN'T SAY a word on the drive back to Philyra, and I was beginning to think this would be the easiest bounty I'd ever brought in…if I didn't get in a fatal car accident along the way. The road was lonely and dark and the rental didn't have auto-drive, didn't even have the night vision heads-up display you found on most ground vehicles, just regular headlights like we were in the damned middle ages or something.

Even Dog was quiet, for a wonder, and I worried about falling asleep at the wheel, but finally the lights of the city shown in the distance, fading out the stars.

"For a small, colony town," I said to Dog, trying to keep myself awake, "Philyra has quite the light pollution problem, doesn't it?"

"It won't last." Beckett had answered instead of Dog, and I risked a look back at her, eyebrows raising, inviting her to go on. She was staring at the town beneath hooded eyes, something dark in her expression. "If there's a profit to be made from people being here, eventually, the big corporations will move in and buy out the smallholders in places like this. And with the corporations will come their workers and executives, and they'll vote in their own representatives and make their own laws and regulations and there'll be no more light pollution, no target practice in the desert, no riding off-road vehicles, no internal combustion engines, no harvesting local wood and everything will be made from imported plastic."

"You don't like regulations, Ms. Beckett?" I asked her. I usually didn't encourage small-talk from folks I was bringing in, but I have to admit, she intrigued me.

"I suppose some of it is necessary when you have more people living close by each other," she allowed, not sounding happy about the admission, "but there should be someplace a person can go and not have everything close up around them."

"I live out of a ship," I told her. "Things get too crowded, hyperspace goes in every direction."

"If I'd actually committed the crimes I'm being accused of," she said so quietly I almost didn't hear it, "I'd have bought a ship and found somewhere I didn't have to live around other people."

"Jean-Paul Sartre said 'hell is other people,'" Dog commented. "Being non-human, I definitely agree."

"Dog!" I snapped, glaring at him. "For God's sake!"

"Did your robot just quote philosophy at me?" Beckett asked, her voice tinged with disbelief.

"It's just an automated response system," I ad-libbed quickly. "I keep meaning to shut it off…"

"Oh, get over yourself, Masterson," Dog scoffed. "Who's she gonna tell?"

"Holy shit," Beckett gasped. I looked in the rear-view mirror and saw her gaping at me. "He's AI, isn't he? How the hell did you get your hands on an AI-equipped robot?"

"It's a long story." It wasn't. I was lying. It was a short story involving a lot of money changing hands between me and bad people I would have arrested if I was still a Marshal, but she didn't *need* to know that any more than she needed to know Dog was an AI. "And sometimes I think he's more of an Artificial Stupid than an Artificial Intelligence."

Dog laughed.

"But how…," Beckett persisted.

"We're at the spaceport," I interrupted, nodding ahead to the fences separating the business offices from the landing field. "If you promise to stay quiet and not cause any trouble, I'll keep you with me while I turn in the rental car instead of locking you in the spare cabin on the ship with no air conditioning."

It wasn't particularly hot at night, but it did get stuffy on the ship, so I was hoping she wouldn't make me walk her all the way out to the *Charietto* and then all the way back to the rental office.

"Sure," she assented, shrugging her disinterest, the temporary fascination at Dog's computer systems seeming to have faded. "What difference does it make?"

The rental office was still open, which was a wonder. Most of them close down at sunset in towns like Philyra, leaving you to an automated kiosk to finish your business, but maybe they figured keeping the employees around was cheaper than maintaining the computer systems. The lights were dim and the middle-aged man behind the counter looked as if he'd rather be having dental surgery than working the desk after dark. He didn't even seem to notice the restraints on Beckett, didn't mention Dog standing next to me, just took my key cards for the rental and tapped the pertinent data into the terminal with an expression of perfect boredom. The name tag on his chest read "Chad."

"It'll be charged to your account," Chad recited to me, reading off a company script. "The receipt will show up in your messages. Colony Rental Services hopes you had a positive experience and will do business with us again."

"I'm certain of it," I assured him, checking my 'link to make sure they hadn't overcharged me.

"Masterson!" Dog said, coming to an alert stance, his whole body pointing out toward the exit.

"For God's sake, why do you have to keep talking?" I exploded before the significance of his posture actually dawned on me. "What?"

"Military-grade Bartoli crystals," he said, his tone clipped and businesslike. "Heading this way."

I grabbed Beckett by the arm and pulled her back toward the counter, shoving the startled clerk in front of us.

"Back entrance, Dog!" I told him. "Find it!"

"What the hell is going on?" Beckett demanded, but I didn't bother to answer just yet.

Military-grade Bartoli crystals were only used for one thing: weapons, *heavy* weapons. Someone was bringing heavy blasters in through the rental return parking lot, and I didn't think it was because they had a negative experience with their Colonial Rental Services vehicle. It could have been the military. The thought pinballed through my head while I was pushing Delia Beckett and the rental clerk down the narrow hallway from the reception area into the tiny employee section of the office, and I supposed it was barely possible. The Navy might have caught wind of Beckett's location from my inquiries and maybe some hard charger in Naval Criminal Investigation Services had sent a contingent of MPs after her.

But I wasn't about to gamble all of our lives on the likelihood someone in the military had suddenly decided to get efficient. Dog led me to a rear exit and the clerk was about to grab the handle and open it when Dog snapped at his wrist, growling and baring his teeth.

Now he gets in character, after everyone and his brother hears him talk.

"What is it?" I asked him, taking a moment to draw my blaster. The clerk's eyes went wide at the sight of the gun.

"They have someone out back," Dog told me. "Two someones unless it's one big fucker carrying two military assault guns."

"Need to work on your language, Dog," I said with a disappointed tsk. I nudged the clerk with my elbow to bring his eyes away from the muzzle of my blaster and up to my face. "Any other exits?"

He shook his head, a jerky motion that sent sweat spattering in every direction. I scowled when I felt a drop hit me in the face.

"Then I guess one of us is about to have a very bad day." I nodded to Dog. "Where?"

"At your two o'clock and eleven, about two meters away."

"Why is the dog talking?" the clerk wondered, fear warring with fascination in his expression.

"Because I can't get him to shut up."

I shoved the door open and threw myself into a shoulder roll, a kaleidoscope of color and neon light and dark sky flashing across my vision, but my focus on the two spots where I knew the people were waiting with guns to try to kill me. I had just the briefest flash of an image, shadowed figures wearing dark, civilian clothing, work coveralls, inobtrusive, designed to blend in. The big-assed assault blasters not so much.

They fired reflexively at the opening of the door and the flare of the military-grade blasters was blinding, ripping apart the night before smashing gaping, blackened craters in the side of the building, nearly penetrating walls built thick enough to hold off the seasonal dust storms. What they would do to me didn't bear consideration and I wasn't going to give them a chance to aim. I didn't much like killing people. Not that some people don't deserve to die, particularly those doing their best to kill me, but it's something you can't take back and I try to avoid it those times I can.

This was not one of those times. Hitting two targets seventy degrees apart from my back at night was tough enough without trying anything trickier than center mass. The blaster was a blunt instrument, a hammer-blow of plasma, one shot each to the chest. Military-grade hard body armor might have stopped the shots, but that would have been conspicuous and these boys had been going for covert until the time had come to break out the big guns. If they wore anything beneath their coveralls, it wasn't enough. They dropped like puppets with their strings cut, the distinctive smell of burned skin and burning clothes wafting through the air along with the dust. I considered grabbing one of their weapons, rejected it just as quickly. They might be biometrically locked and I wouldn't have time to let Dog work his magic on them.

"Bring her," I rasped quietly, trusting Dog to hear me.

I'd formed a picture of the back of the office in my head before I made my move and I knew exactly where we were going. We could make it quick and quiet, and maybe the guys out front wouldn't even know where we'd gone, if we were lucky…

"Oh, my fucking God! You killed them! You killed them! Oh, Jesus!"

I'd forgotten about Chad.

"Go!" I yelled, sprinting for the rental car storage lot. "Get us into one of them, Dog!"

Delia Beckett stumbled into me, nearly losing her footing when Dog let her sleeve loose from his teeth and dashed ahead of us, a barely visible streak of tan fur. I grabbed her around the shoulders and kept both of us on our feet and running across the pavement, half lifting her off the ground when we jumped over the decorative anchor-chain fence between the employee lot and the rentals.

"Untie my damned hands!" she yelled in my ear.

Sure, let me just stop right here in the middle of the lot and let them shoot us while I do that.

I said nothing, just aimed straight where I'd seen Dog running, hoping he wasn't going to be too picky when it came to finding a vehicle to break into. Blaster-fire sounded behind us, high, whining snap-cracks echoing in the halls of the rental office and I hoped Chad had enough sense to run. I couldn't take responsibility for every dumbass who lacks the sense to come in out of the rain, but these guys were here for me, not him.

The interior lights came on in a boxy utility vehicle two rows away from us, past a line of low-slung sportsters. I dragged Beckett with me, squeezing between the rows and yanking the passenger's side rear door open, pushing her inside and ducking around the back of the vehicle and trying to climb into the driver's seat. Dog was sitting there, one paw resting on the security plate.

"Move over!" I urged him, feeling an itch between my shoulder blades where I expected the blaster bolt to hit.

"No can do," he insisted. "I can only keep this thing going by maintaining a direct connection to the security plate." He jerked his head toward the passenger's seat. "Get in. I'll drive."

"I'm never gonna live this down," I muttered, scrambling around the front of the car this time and jumping in just as the vehicle peeled out of the parking spot, barely getting my door closed in time to avoid hitting the rover parked next to us.

"The dog is driving?" Beckett asked. I twisted around to look back at the rental car office and saw three men piling out of the back door.

"Get down!" I yelled at Beckett, shoving her sideways in the seat just before a stuttering line of incandescent flashes streaked out from the rear door and chewed through the rear right corner of the boxy utility vehicle.

Burning plastic and metal spewed across the cabin and I threw up a hand and ducked down, cursing as a spark scored my right cheek. The car was fishtailing hard, the engine revving with effort, and the skewing motion threw me into the door shoulder-first, jostling the blaster from my hand, sending it clattering to the floorboards.

"You might want to strap in," Dog suggested, his tone maddeningly calm.

"You drive more like a dog than a robot." I yanked the safety harness across my chest and buckled it tight, then thought of Beckett and yelled over my shoulder. "Stay on the floor and keep your head down."

Dog had turned onto the main road, wheeling the car off to the left and turning our nose back at the spaceport. I tried to reach the gun on the floor, but a sudden slam on the brakes to avoid a running pedestrian brought me up short, the seat harness grabbing me tight enough to squeeze the breath out of my chest. I saw Chad's pale and puffy face frozen in our headlights for just a moment before Dog blew the horn and the rental clerk bolted away, running headlong across the street and into the wilderness.

Dog hit the accelerator again and we surged forward just ahead of another blaster burst, the flare of ionized atmosphere lighting up the interior, turning the smoke still drifting from the last hit into a glowing fog. It was just as well Dog was driving because I couldn't see a damn thing, and I wasn't sure which way we were heading until the chain-link fence was looming right in front of us, the pedestrian gate just a centimeter too narrow for our vehicle.

Metal scraped and polymer ripped and the engine screamed and the whole vehicle shuddered until it yanked free, delivered like a baby through the birth canal…or another, more scatological analogy that came to mind. Dog was becoming a bad influence.

"The port police are going to be all over us driving out here without authorization," I pointed out, finally able to bend down and retrieve my blaster off the floor.

"I'm of the opinion police protection might be desirable. They're following us."

My neck was getting sore from staring behind us, but I could see the headlights following us out through the forcefully widened gate, whipping back and forth as they squeezed and scraped their way out onto the plain of the spaceport.

"You can outrun them, right?" I asked him. "Can we go any faster?"

"You notice that shimmying on the right side of the car?" Dog replied to my question with one of his own. In fact, I had, but I just thought it had been the rough road, or perhaps his driving. "Well, that's the front wheel about to come off this thing from hitting the fence. I'll keep it going as long as I can."

"Well, darn."

I rolled down the passenger's side window, unlatched my seat belt and leaned out, trying to draw a bead on the vehicle trailing us. I'd just about compensated for the shuddering, swaying motion of the car when lightning cracked out of the passenger's side of the car behind us and passed half a meter from my head. I jerked back inside, biting down on a curse.

"These boys are persistent."

"Who the hell did you piss off this time?" Dog wondered.

"They're after me," Beckett declared.

Her voice was muffled, and I peeked over the seat, making sure I'd heard her right.

"They're after me," she repeated. "You should let them have me. No one else needs to get killed because of me."

I wanted to argue with her, wanted to question further why she might think that, but we were coming up on the port, coming close to the slot where the *Charietto* had landed, and we weren't going to have the time or space to board her with these guys on our ass. I lunged back out of the window and started firing before I'd even tried to sight in, just walking the actinic plasma across the pavement in a long, draining burst until it intersected the utility rover's front right wheel.

Sparks showered off melting metal and shredded plastic flared in a brief gout of flame just before my blaster went dead, its charge gone. It was enough. The rover nosed into the pavement, spinning out and flipping onto its roof with a screeching crash that set my teeth on edge.

"Good shooting for a meatsack," Dog complimented. "And just in time."

The *Charietto* squatted in resentful silence, an angry, silver wedge over a hundred meters long and half that wide, battered and worn from decades of use before she became mine, I'd sunken everything I had into her and she was still costing me over half of every bounty I brought in. Normally, the thought of the money outlay gave me a bit of heartburn, but this time I was just happy as hell to see her.

Dog wasn't using the manual controls, just operating them through a direct computer connection, so when he slammed on the brakes, there was absolutely no warning. The car slid sideways across the bow of the ship and screeched to a stop, bouncing fitfully on the suspension. I was already jammed against the door, so I simply pulled the handle and tumbled out of it, rolling into a crouch. My blaster's charge pack was drained and I took a moment to swap it for a fresh one, tucking the spent pack into my jacket pocket before I opened the rear door and helped Beckett out.

She was cursing loudly with each tug toward the door, clearly unhappy about being tossed around in the rear seat with her hands secured behind her back, but I wasn't going to waste time setting her loose, not when two of the gunmen were crawling out of the wreck of their truck and probably only seconds from opening fire on us again. Dog was out of the car and he had the hatch opening already, the interior lights throwing out an elongated halo of yellow in the particulate wind.

The ramp crawled downward in slow motion and it took quite

a bit of self-control not to urge it along with useless profanity. I raised my blaster to shoulder level and fired off two quick bursts towards the overturned vehicle, trying to force the two men I'd seen near it to keep their heads down. There were sirens in the distance and when I checked around the other side of the *Chari-etto*, I could see the flashing lights of the approaching vehicles. Just groundcars, not even a flyer. Philyra was really a backwoods sort of place.

"Port cops," Dog said, staring at the hatch, waiting for it to unfold. When it was halfway down, he leapt inside with an impossible bound…impossible for a flesh-and-blood dog, that is.

"Maybe we should just wait for them to get here," I mused aloud, more of an argument with myself than a request for advice, but Delia Beckett made a face at me like I'd grown an extra head. "Oh, I know, I'd likely wind up spending a day in jail while they sort through everything, but the alternative is leaving two dead bodies lying around and never being able to come back here again."

I shut up, not because I was tired of hearing myself talk, but because a whining in my ear made me look up. I couldn't see the aircraft at first, just heard the jets, but I knew what it was: a VTOL flyer coming in from the direction of town. That, in and of itself, was nothing strange. Flyers probably landed at the port's public lots all the time, a quick way for people to jet in from the outback. But this one didn't seem to be running any safety lights, and it was coming in nap-of-the-earth, low enough to stay off the port radar.

"Oh, boy," I said.

The ramp was unfolding its final segment, but I didn't wait for it, just lifted Beckett onto the lowest set of steps and gave her a shove. She nearly stumbled but put her shoulder against the safety rail and lunged upward, tumbling into the utility bay. I jumped and grabbed the railings, vaulting over the last section of steps as they swung down at me, and climbing the rest of the ladder up to the deck.

I risked a look back at the approaching port police vehicles, only about a hundred and fifty meters away now, throwing up a dust cloud that glowed with a polychromatic halo from their emergency lights. They'd be here in seconds and I'd have some explaining to do...

The blaster fire exploded out of the night, the chin cannon tucked close against the fuselage of the unlit flyer, only the brief flares of plasma revealing its sleek, dagger-shaped lines. Stuttering red bolts drifted toward the path of the police cars in a long, walking burst and my gut clenched in sympathy as they intersected the first of the vehicles. Eye-searing yellow and white blossomed up from the police car, leaving a trail of brilliant sparks and billowing flame and smoke as the vehicle veered out of control off to my left, rumbling to a stop.

The second car tried to swerve, tried to evade, but there was no way to outrun a blaster cannon. All the swerving and dodging accomplished was to tip the thing over when the bursts finally walked their way across the left-side wheel base. And now that it was done with them, the flyer would be coming for us.

[6]

"Dog!" I yelled, slamming the lever to fold the ramp back up, running past where Delia Beckett was sprawled out on the deck, trying to squirm to her feet. "Get us out of here!"

But the ship was already lurching upwards, nearly sending me sprawling with the abrupt motion. I caught myself on the bulkhead of the narrow passageway between the utility bay and the cockpit, pushing away and sprinting the last few meters before I had the chance to fall again. Dog was in the right seat, leaving the left for me, thoughtfully allowing me the illusion I was still the captain of this boat.

I strapped in, knowing I should have tried to help Beckett into a safe position but also knowing it was better for her to be a little banged up than it was for all of us to get burned to ashes if that flyer managed to get a lucky shot into us before we could get up to speed. I thought I might have heard her pained squawk somewhere back down the passage when the *Charietto's* atmospheric drives rumbled to life and pushed me back into the acceleration couch.

"Civilian Transport CT-823701," an annoyed voice came over the cockpit speakers as the ground dropped away beneath the front screens, "this is Philyra Traffic Control. You do not have clearance to take off. Please return to your slip and request clearance."

"Slip," I murmured. "It ain't a slip, it's a parking space." I touched the communications control to activate the cockpit audio pickup. "Philyra Control, this is an emergency. Criminals have attacked port police near our ship, there are several casualties and we have to evacuate the area. You need to send emergency services immediately."

The exasperated sigh was a burst of static against the man's microphone. "823701, drop the bullshit and return to your slip immediately or you're going to be facing a possible five-thousand-credit fine and impoundment of your ship!"

"Where's the flyer?" I asked Dog, muting the communications pickup.

"It broke off once our atmospheric drives kicked in," he reported, staring at the control panel as if there were a movie playing on it. I knew he was hooked into the ship's computer system, monitoring sensors, satellite communications and our flight data. "Traffic control is trying to send a remote shutdown sequence to the ship's flight computer," he added. "I'm not letting them do that."

"And don't think I don't appreciate it." I threw off my seat restraints and climbed out of the acceleration couch as our flight began to steady. "I'm going to go see to our guest. Let me know if the police send out intercept craft."

"We're never going to be able to come back here, you know," Dog called after me.

I grunted agreement, but didn't respond. Like all the disasters in my life, I couldn't think how I would have reacted differently to this one.

I found Beckett huddled on the deck in the utility bay, her leg wrapped around the support strut for the work table and a nascent bruise already rising on her cheek where she'd banged against something.

"Sorry about that," I told her, helping her to her feet and pulling her along to the cockpit. "Had to get us out of there before they decided to take a run at us."

"They aren't going to give up," she warned me, not seeming to begrudge the bruising, not even complaining about the restraints. "They waited this long, the only reason they came after me now is that you found me. They won't give up until I'm dead."

"Who the heck is this 'they' you keep talking about, ma'am?" I asked pulling out a multi-tool and cutting the flex-cuffs off of her as we walked.

She rubbed at her wrists but didn't say anything until I'd guided her to the unoccupied navigation console and strapped her in. I paused and pulled another set of flex-cuffs out of my pocket and secured her right wrist to the chair's armrest. By the time I turned around and began buckling my own restraints, the low clouds above Morrigan had given way to star-filled blackness.

"Masterson." Dog's voice was flat, with no inflection, a warning tone. "There's a ship coming in."

"Orbital Patrol?" I asked, suddenly concerned. I couldn't even remember if the planetary law enforcement here had armed ships and I silently calculated how long it would take us to safe jump range and whether we could outrun a fusion-drive orbital cutter.

"I don't think so. It's a starship, personal transport just like this one. No official registration so it's not military or police."

"Maybe it's just doing a normal orbital insertion," I suggested, trying to bring up the sensor screen so I could see what he was getting directly from the computer.

"It's on an intercept course."

"Well, that's not a coincidence." I twisted around to look back at Beckett. "Come clean, lady. Who are these guys?"

"No time for that now," Dog chided me. "These assholes wouldn't be homing in on us if they didn't have the guns to back it up. You want to call the local Navy base for help?"

"Head for the closest safe jump point," I told him, bringing up the communications screen on the console between us and trying to find the emergency broadcast frequency. "Union Navy Operations," I called. "Any Navy forces, this is CT-823701 declaring an emergency. We need help now. Please respond."

There was nothing. I repeated the call and then began scrolling through trouble-shooting screens before Dog saved me the trouble.

"We're being jammed."

Jamming civil communications signals wasn't easy, and it wasn't cheap. And anyone who had the gear to pull it off and weren't afraid of getting caught were not to be trifled with. I reached beneath the edge of the command console and flipped up a hidden control panel with a targeting screen and a joystick. A remotely-controlled blaster turret popped down from the chin of the *Charietto* at the touch of a button. Technically, it's not legal even for a licensed bounty hunter to have anti-ship weaponry… but then, technically, Dog was illegal enough to get me life in prison. In for a penny, in for a pound.

"They'll be in range in ten seconds," Dog advised me. "Range for *us*. I don't know what the hell they're shooting with."

A good point. If they had torpedoes, we were dead and nothing was going to change it. I pivoted the turret around and tried to target the sensor icon representing their ship. It wasn't quite visible yet, just a shining dot reflecting the starlight from Epsilon Indi. Morrigan basked in the starshine as the terminator passed beneath us, brown and blue and white and green, looking so much more hospitable now than when we'd flown in.

"How long before we jump?"

By way of answer, the roar of the main drive went an octave

higher and twice my normal weight pressed me into the acceleration couch, which wasn't comfortable but wasn't exactly debilitating. We'd done six-gee accelerations before, and *those* were truly miserable.

"Five minutes at two gees," Dog told me. "Unless you want to push it harder. It'll play hell with our fuel supply, though."

"No, this is enough. Just jump us out of here and head back to the Panicle as quick as you can."

I wasn't paying attention to what was ahead of us, instead fixated on the ship coming up behind us. It was visible in the optical cameras, a delta-winged, silver wedge in the targeting screen, like looking into a mirror image of the *Charietto*. My thumb flexed with an involuntary urge to fire on them preemptively, to get them the second they came into range, but I restrained myself.

"Shoot them down!" Beckett urged, the view on my screen visible from her position. "Hurry!"

"They haven't fired on us," I reminded her, just a hint of the strain of the two-gravity fusion burn coming through in my voice. "If I blow them to vapors and it turns out they weren't armed, or, worse yet, aren't even with those people who attacked us at the port, I'll be spending the better part of the next twenty or thirty years at a government work camp."

The argument became moot when a scintillating stream of red energy flashed out from the chin of the other ship and splashed against the stern in a shower of sparks and a halo of sublimating metal. The *Charietto* lurched with the hit, which seemed wrong to me somehow. Nothing solid had struck her, just a burst of energy, but I knew from unfortunate previous experience the jolt was akin to the one the ship would undergo when it fired maneuvering thrusters and for the same reason: the spray of burning metal was acting as a brief and violent steering jet.

I only cared about the science of it so far as it affected

whether I lived or died in the next few seconds. The flare of burning gas obscured the view in the targeting screen for the briefest of moments and by the time it was clear, Dog was already throwing the *Charietto* into an evasion pattern, tossing me back and forth against my seat restraints and sending the image on the display jumping all over the place. More crimson slashes of fire streaked across our port side only a few dozen meters away, seeking us out, trying to finish us off and, above the roar of the engines and the bang-bang-bang of maneuvering thrusters, I could hear Beckett saying "Jesus, Jesus, Jesus…." I wasn't sure if it was a profanity or a prayer.

Gee forces were fighting against my hand on the turret control joystick but I grabbed my right wrist with my left and steadied it as best I could, gently traversing the gun turret and moving the targeting camera back around to the silver delta.

"Shoot the fucker, will you?" Dog snapped.

I was thumbing the trigger even as he spoke, which bothered me since I didn't want him to think he could boss me around… and because it worked. The burst took the silver delta just starboard of its nose, scoring a jagged black line ten meters down the length of the fuselage and throwing it off to the port in an uncontrolled yaw. I tried to traverse around to follow them, but the turret reached the limit of its firing arc.

"How much longer?" I asked through clenched teeth, swinging the gun back and forth, trying to find him again.

"Two minutes," Dog told me, as cool as ever, as if the possibility of being blown up didn't greatly disturb him. "But there are energy fluctuations in the drive matrix. I think we took some damage from that hit. Can't promise she'll hold together for the jump."

"You'd rather stick around here?"

"I'm just letting you know. You're theoretically in charge."

There, there it was again, flashing across my display moving across our course from starboard to port. I twisted the joystick and tried to catch up with him, firing reflexively before I even had a target lock. Glowing red traces of energy chased after him, raw power from our reactor funneled through Bartoli crystals and focused into bursts of plasma, but he was moving too fast. They had to be accelerating at five or six gravities, trying to outpace us, trying to get in front of our course and face us nose-on.

The ability to keep control of the ship under a high-gee boost meant the pilot probably had military experience. That meant mercenaries, not just ordinary, everyday gun thugs. I already knew they were ruthless and well-equipped. All of it together smelled like money, and lots of it. Whoever was trying to kill Beckett, if she was indeed the target, was connected. Organized crime at the least. At the most…well, there were always men like Tomas Caty.

The targeting reticle seemed to be dancing all over the screen with every evasive maneuver Dog made, and I blasted more plasma energy off into the black to disperse harmlessly, keeping it to short bursts. Energy wasn't the issue, overheating was. Maybe a Navy cruiser could spray blaster fire for ten or twenty seconds at a time and count on redundant Bartoli crystals to hold up, but if I poured too much power through the turret in too short a time, my crystals were going to overheat and crack and that would be all she wrote.

"Port!" Dog warned me and I slewed the turret around.

They hit first. The jolt was stronger this time, more hull armor sublimated to the vacuum, enough that Dog had to hit the maneuvering jets to correct the oversteer. Red lights were flashing warnings about hull breaches and structural integrity and every one of them just seemed like more and more money flying right out of my bank account. I caught a glimpse of a target in the gun reticle and punched the trigger like it was to blame for all my troubles. I nearly missed, would have if the other pilot hadn't jinked the wrong direction, trying to outguess me, and rolled right into a burst of star-hot plasma. I couldn't have made that shot if I'd tried, but fortune, as they say, favors the bold, and God smiles on children and the simple-minded. Crimson energy exploded away from the other ship's portside wing and he finally broke off, backing down his acceleration and falling behind us.

"Everyone hold onto something," Dog warned. "We're jumping."

I folded the weapons control panel into the console and frowned at Dog. "Why would we need to hold onto some…?" I started to ask.

Then the stars ahead of us twisted into a rainbow ring in the front viewscreens and reality crumpled me into a wad and threw me screaming into the trash can.

$$[\ 7\ ]$$

"WHAT THE...." I bit down on the curse and fixed Dog with a glare once my vision had cleared. "What happened?"

The main screen had gone dead, but it always did in hyper-space. There was nothing in that dimension either a human or a human-designed Artificial Intelligence could comprehend. I'd jumped dozens of times, both in my law enforcement career and since, and it was usually mildly disconcerting but nothing like what I'd just experienced. I wiped at my nose and my fingers came away with a small trickle of blood. Beckett wasn't bleeding, but she was groaning softly, holding her head in her one free hand. Dog, of course, looked as fresh as a daisy.

"I told you there was an energy fluctuation in the drive," he said with an aggrieved tone, as if it were somehow my fault. "We made it though, didn't we? Just a couple hours to the Panicle."

I regarded Delia Beckett, sitting secured to the navigator's station, recovered from the shock of the rough hyperspace jump now but still seeming miserable and resigned to her fate, as well as nursing a nasty bruise on the side of her head. I unstrapped and clambered out of the cockpit back to the utility bay, pulling open the first aid cabinet. It stuck, battered and abused like everything else on the ship. I'd slowly been fixing up the interior since I'd bought her, but I hadn't had to use the medical gear much, for which I was grateful, and hadn't gotten around to working on the warped, metal hatch.

I pulled out a cold pack and took it back to the cockpit, twisting it to activate the refrigerants inside and handing it to Delia Beckett. She looked from the pack to me for a moment, as if she wasn't sure what it was for, but then took it and pressed it against the side of her face.

"Thanks," she said, her voice still subdued and defensive.

"We need to talk," I told her. "Who wants you dead that bad?"

"I still think they could have been after you," Dog insisted, hopping out of the pilot's seat and padding over beside me. "That asshole Caty could be gunning for you still."

I shook my head. "He already had his revenge. I think he made it pretty clear he'd rather let me live than put me out of my misery."

There was a lot more bitterness in the statement than I'd intended, and I wasn't sure if it had been creeping there beneath the surface after all this time, or if Dog's words had dredged it up from the briny deep. I shook it away and pressed on.

"Those were professionals," I said to Beckett, "mercenaries. Probably ex-military, either from the Union or maybe even from the Confederation Wars. Why would they be after you? Who did you tick off that badly?"

"It's better if you don't know." She leaned into the cold-pack, eyes closing. "It's safer for you."

"Well, obviously fucking not!" Dog pointed out. I disagreed with his language, but not his sentiment.

"Ma'am," I said, trying to keep my tone cool and even despite the onset of the post-fight adrenalin shakes sending a chill right through my core, "they know who I am. They know what this ship is. I am involved, whether or not it was a good idea. I know you don't owe me anything and I'm the guy who just slapped you in handcuffs and hauled you away, but if people are trying to kill us, I would really like to know who they are."

"Can I have some water?" she asked, not meeting my eyes.

I very deliberately did *not* sigh in exasperation, though the temptation was there. Instead, I pulled open a small cooler built into the bulkhead beside the pilot's seat and retrieved a bottle, twisting the lid off before handing it to her. She took her time drinking it and I started getting thirsty just watching her, and then started thinking I needed to pee before chalking both up to incipient shock and settling for a moment's meditation to calm my thoughts.

"When I left Absolution," Beckett said, her eyes still downcast, her voice so soft I could barely hear her, "I went to work for a defense contractor called Hadur Technologies out in the Panicle." My brows knit as I tried to recall the name and she must have noticed. "If you haven't heard of them, don't feel bad. They were one of a couple dozen that sprang up during the Confederation Wars, all of them trying to jump on the gravy train of selling weapons to Danu and Dagda before the Union brokered a peace there. Once the Navy cracked down on arms sales, Hadur began circling the drain like all the rest of them."

She finished the last of the water in a long swallow and her jaw set with what might have been anger, or maybe pain. It was hard to tell the difference sometimes.

"I thought that was it, that I would have to try to find a job with one of the big firms selling to the Union Navy, which would have sucked because the demand is fixed and the jobs are low-paying, but it was either that or start again at the bottom of the ladder. And then Hadur got bought out."

"By who?" I asked, wondering why anyone would bother.

"Whom," Dog corrected.

"Pedant," I murmured. Dog lifted an ear and stared at me.

"You don't know who from whom but you know how to use the word 'pedant?' You get some traumatic brain injury you didn't report to the Marshals back in the day?"

"Who bought out Hadur Technologies?" I asked, side-stepping the grammatical land-mine.

"A corporation calling itself Nautilus Acquisitions Group." She chuckled, as if in bitter admiration. "Cheeky bastards, aren't they?"

I shook my head, not sure why they were cheeky, nor yet sure exactly what "cheeky" meant, and doubly confused as to how their parentage figured into it.

"Nautilus," she repeated, gesturing as if it was obvious.

"They're a *shell* corporation, you big doofus," Dog said, as if that was enough explanation.

"Okay," I prompted, still not getting it but unwilling to further explore my ignorance of the joke. "And how did you figure out they were a shell corporation?"

"Jake. Jacob Wiley, one of my co-workers." The corners of her eyes pinched, just the slightest wince of pain. "He was an engineer and I worked in shipping. We were…involved. I was just happy as hell we still had jobs, that someone was stupid enough to sink money into Hadur. He got suspicious as to why they would bother buying out a sinking defense contractor and he began looking into them. There was nothing there, no interviews, no news reports, no names we could trace to anyone with a record of any kind. They were shadows, specters, nothing you could pin down."

"What did you do?"

"Nothing." She shrugged. "Jake was suspicious, but no one

had done anything wrong and we were still getting paid, so we just kept coming to work. And the orders kept coming in. We had no idea where it was going, but it kept coming in. Not for weapons, but for raw materials, fusion reactor parts, radiation shielding. And Bartoli crystals. Lots and lots of military-grade Bartoli crystals. We had an official license to buy them, of course. We'd never given it up. But we were only allowed to sell them to Union-authorized buyers."

"You weren't selling them, though," I said, beginning to see what she was saying. "You were just shipping them to the company that had bought you out."

"That's how I justified it in my head, at first." She set the cold-pack down, rubbing her hands together to warm up the left one. "But like I said, I was in shipping, and I had to deal with it every month and, eventually, Jake convinced me I needed to find out where the crystals were being sent, that it was our responsibility. He said if someone used them to start a war, or carry out a terrorist attack, it would be our fault."

"And you did find out." It wasn't a question.

"They were shipping them to Hanuman, one of the moons of Agni, right here in the Epsilon Indi system. But there were no records of them being shipped out from their facilities on Hanuman to anywhere else, or of sales to anyone. Which made no sense. No one is going to pay hundreds of millions of credits for that many military-grade Bartoli crystals just to stick them in a warehouse on some nowhere moon in a backwater system like Epsilon Indi. Something was going on."

"And this is where everything goes horribly wrong, I'm assuming," Dog surmised.

"Jake wanted to go to the Marshals straight off," she said, sniffling and wiping at her nose with the back of her hand. "Just give them everything we had, tell them our suspicions and let the chips fall where they may. But I didn't want to lose my job. I knew I wouldn't find another this good, and Jake and I would probably have to separate in order to find work. So, instead, I went to the head of my department, Deborah Modi. I'd known her for years…we were friends. I thought she'd be safe, thought she'd know the right thing to do."

Her whole body seemed to clench like a fist, as if she was trying to pin something inside that wouldn't be contained, and finally the sobs broke through.

"I came home that day and found Jake's body in our apartment." Her voice broke and her face quivered as she fought to keep going. "He'd been stabbed with a knife I inherited from my father, one he used to use when we would go camping together." She squeezed her eyes shut, pushing the heels of her hands into them to scrub away the memories. "There was so much blood…"

I gave her a moment. It cost nothing to be considerate, and if I was in a hurry to find out what was going on, well, waiting for her to compose herself and not rushing her wouldn't cost me that much time.

"I called the Marshals *then*. Too late. Modi must have told them, told this Nautilus Group, given them time to set things up. When the authorities arrived, it wasn't the Marshals, it was the Military Police, and they arrested me for murder, which would have been a local jurisdictional matter, as well as treason and misappropriation of vital military assets, which were not. They made it look as if Jake and I had hatched the whole plan, authorized the purchase and smuggling out of the Bartoli crystals."

"How the hell did you escape the MPs?" I wanted to know. I wasn't sure if I believed her version of the events—I'd dealt with criminals my whole life and every single one of them was innocent if you asked them—but I really was curious as to how they'd let her get away.

She shrugged it off as if it were the least interesting part of the story. "The MPs had locked me up in the holding cell down in corporate security while they searched my workstation and collected more evidence from my apartment. It took them hours."

Her teeth clenched at the memory. I could sympathize, having been there. Hours of fear and dread and tedium and nothing to do but think about how badly you'd screwed up.

"It was gradually beginning to sink in what was happening, how they'd set all this up in so short a time, and I had to think they'd seen it coming, maybe when Jake and I first started looking into Nautilus. I was scared, panicking. They were about to take me to the Navy base and then, from there, I'd be held at the military prison back in the Solar System while I awaited trial. The MPs had left a couple of guards watching the cell, because I guess they didn't trust corporate security." Her brow knitted, still confused after all this time. "Something happened. I still don't understand the why of it all, and there was no one I could ask, obviously. But there was a power failure in the cell block and they had to go check it out and try to see why backups hadn't come on. And the door was suddenly unlocked. Someone wanted me to get away, and I did."

She motioned off-handedly, as if everything else was an afterthought. "I made it to El Mercado and got work on a grey-market freighter heading out to Morrigan. It was too easy, but I wasn't in jail so I didn't think about it too hard."

"So, you think whoever is behind Nautilus hired these mercenaries to come after you when they heard I was going to bring you in?" I tapped my fingers against the edge of the control panel, fitting the timeline together. "They could have had a worm in the Fugitive Retrieval database to notify them if someone picked up the bounty. Or that local yokel cop could have been on the take."

I leaned against the command console and tried to think with my head instead of my heart. Because my heart *wanted* to believe her. Her story sounded way too familiar and I couldn't let myself make another huge mistake just because I wanted what she said to be true.

"Whether you buy all this or not," Dog said, as if he were reading my thoughts, "the way she escaped is all kinds of fishy. Something's going on here, Grant."

"Is there any evidence?" I asked her. "Anything you could get your hands on to prove what you're saying?" I sounded almost as desperate as her, and maybe I was.

"There's something," she admitted, the words almost prying their way free of her. "But it's not...I can't use it. The penalty for using it would be as high as the one I'm already facing."

That tossed all my thoughts up in the air and scrambled them, but she wouldn't say another word on the matter. I stared at her for a long minute, trying to decide what to do.

"You know," Dog suggested slowly, almost hesitantly, which I knew was an affectation since he never has to hesitate about anything, "that moon, Hanuman, is just a couple hours away through hyperspace. We could go check it out ourselves. Wouldn't take too long at all." His ears flicked in the equivalent of a shrug. "From there, it's just a short hop back to the Panicle."

I nodded. I liked the idea. At the very least, whether she was innocent as a newborn babe or guilty as sin, we might have a better handle on the identity of the people who were gunning for us.

"Hanuman is a closed facility," I reminded him. "It's a corporate business park, automated mining equipment and the people who service it, plus a few research labs and all of it's restricted access. What excuse could we give for being there?"

"We don't have to make up an excuse," Dog reminded me. "Damaged hyperdrive, remember? Honestly, a couple more jumps without fixing it and we might just wind up scattered all over two universes."

"Well, aren't you just full of good news?" I muttered. I knew I could sit on that console till we reached the Panicle and still not have any better or more logical reason to go through with this other than my gut. "All right, Dog. Maybe I'm crazy, but I don't like getting shot at, and I want to make somebody sorry they tried it. Set a course for Hanuman."

[8]

HANUMAN WAS A WORLD OF ANGRY, seething red pustules against a sullen yellow, harsh to look at and even harsher to try to survive. The sensors told the story, even if I hadn't already known. The atmosphere was mostly sulphur dioxide, sucked away gradually by the gravity of Agni and replenished by an incredible amount of geological activity. Agni was a truculent orange and red god staring down at his wayward child, keeping him too close for too long.

The *Charietto* shuddered as she passed through the spot where the gravity from Hanuman began to outstrip the pull from Agni, and I was reminded how unhealthy the radiation from the gas giant was supposed to be if you were exposed to it for too long without shielding. Which is, I suppose, why the helium mines in its atmosphere were automated.

"You ever been here before?" Dog wondered.

I was surprised he'd asked. He had access to most of my history with the Marshals, but I supposed there were some parts still classified due to sensitive government data.

"Never had the pleasure. But Larry did. He was out here for a murder investigation once, something too hot for the local corporate security to handle." I turned back to Beckett, who was still in the navigator's position, though no longer handcuffed. I hadn't seen the point, since Dog would have ripped her throat out if she tried anything with the ship. "Larry was my old partner in the Marshals," I elaborated.

"You were with the Marshals?" She seemed surprised. "What happened?"

I winced, feeling as if I'd been slapped. It wasn't the memories she'd brought up, just the casual assumption that a bounty hunter had to be some scapegrace with a tragic backstory.

Well, aren't you?

"I made the mistake of thinking the law applied to everyone." The words came casual, as if there was no emotional baggage hanging off of them. I'd gotten pretty good at that over the past couple years. "And I wouldn't take no for an answer."

The communications board lit up with an incoming signal and I leaned over to activate the cockpit speakers. Static crackled for a half-second before the voice came through.

"Unidentified civilian craft, you are approaching restricted space. You need to adjust course immediately and leave the area."

"They all sound exactly alike," I mused. "Every traffic control coordinator I've ever heard could have been the same guy."

"That's because half of them are the same AI program," Dog told me. "And the other half try to imitate him."

"Hanuman Traffic Control," I broadcast, leaning over the audio pickup, "this is the civilian transport *Charietto* declaring an emergency and requesting immediate clearance to land. Our hyperdrive is malfunctioning and if we try to jump anywhere else, it's likely going to rip us to atoms."

"Wait one, *Charietto*."

He sounded annoyed and I was guessing this was a human imitating the aforementioned AI program. AI's of sufficient complexity *could* get annoyed, Dog was proof of that, but you weren't going to waste time and money buying an anthropomorphic sentient program when one that could fake it was just as workable.

"Do you think they'll...," Beckett blurted, but I shushed her with a finger over my lips and a pained look. I hadn't turned off the audio pickup.

"*Charietto*, you have clearance to land at Commercial Platform Three. Follow the signal in and do not deviate or you will be reported to the Navy. If you attempt to land anywhere else, the locks will not be opened for you and you will not be allowed to dock. Once you land, wait for the docking umbilical and allow our inspection team on board before trying to disembark. Please acknowledge."

"Hanuman Control, instructions acknowledged," I said. "We will stick to your flight plan, and thanks very much for the help."

I very visibly cut the connection before I turned back to Dog and Beckett.

"I guess they take their security seriously out here," I allowed. "Take us down, Dog. And make our systems nice and presentable in case they check them."

"Yeah, yeah," Dog rolled his eyes before turning back to the controls. "What the hell do I keep you around for, anyway?"

"Because you can't talk without someone putting a blaster shot through you," I reminded him.

"Okay, I'll give you that one."

The descent through the atmosphere was both quicker than usual and more energy intensive, since there wasn't much atmosphere to descend through. Not as much friction but not as much lift and not as much input to the turbines, so we were boosting most of the way down on the plasma drives, burning way too much fuel for my frugal tastes. The featureless wasteland of Hanuman clarified with proximity, cracks opening and broadening, outgassing from hundreds of volcanic cones pumping sulfur dioxide into the air and, eventually, out of the atmosphere to the faint ring around Agni.

The course we'd been given by the navigational signal took us only a dozen kilometers or so past one of the volcanos, jagged and seething, the glow of a single red eye burning through the haze of gas at its apex. Down twenty or thirty kilometers from the base of the mound were the mines. Not gas separators like the ones in Agni's atmosphere, these stripped ore from the ground the old-fashioned way, with massive excavators and an endless chain of cargo buckets riding a conveyor into the smelting plant. Man-made volcanos right beside the natural kind, and if there was anything good to say about the brutal, industrial inelegance of it all, at least it wasn't tearing up a living planet.

Nothing lived here, not even the hardiest extremophiles, not even in the warmth of the volcanic vents. Only humans, tucked safely inside their climate-conditioned caves, braved this hostile moon, and only because training and supporting human workers was still cheaper than paying the exorbitant government licenses for the sentient AI to do the same job.

Which, I guess, is the point of those exorbitant license fees. All some well-intentioned attempt to keep humans relevant. Probably doomed, like everything else government tried to socially engineer.

The colony itself was small, more of an industrial park than a settlement, a handful of domes affixed to quake-proof platforms on hydraulic support columns. Barely bigger in all than Absolution, though spread out further, connected by pressurized cylindrical passageways. The landing platforms were broad and circular, each marked with a number large enough to see from the air a kilometer away, and only one was currently occupied, with what looked like a conventional orbital shuttle. I figured they kept it on hand for trips to whatever orbital transfer vehicle took them to the gas mining stations in Agni's atmosphere for maintenance visits.

We landed gently on platform three, as ordered, the belly jets kicking up sprays of burning sulfur powder deposited there by the volcano. Dog killed the ship's field generator and the local gravity kicked in with an almost euphoric lightness, maybe a third of a standard gee. I was careful not to spring up too quickly when I removed my flight harness, not wanting to fetch up against the overhead like some greenhorn who'd never been anywhere but a space station before.

"Docking umbilical is raising up out of the platform," Dog said.

"Don't talk," I warned Beckett. "They're going to be suspicious enough, so let's keep it simple. I'm a bounty hunter, because I can't hide my ship registration. You're Rebecca Mitchell and you're apprenticing with me. We were attacked by raiders in orbit around Morrigan and jumped here out of desperation. Got it?"

She nodded, but that wasn't going to be enough under the circumstances.

"No, repeat it back to me," I insisted.

"I'm Rebecca Mitchell," she said, "your apprentice. We got attacked by raiders at Morrigan and jumped here by accident."

Something was sparkling in her eyes, something I hadn't seen in them before. It might have been hope. I didn't bother telling her it was premature. *Let her enjoy it while she can.*

When the inner airlock opened, the three of us were lined up waiting for it like we were posing for a family portrait, trying to look as innocent and harmless as possible. The three, armed security guards who emerged from the lock didn't seem as if they were buying it.

"Whose ship is this?" their leader demanded, glancing back and forth between Beckett and me, beady, dark eyes sheltered under brows that might have come straight from his Neanderthal ancestors. He hadn't drawn his blaster, but his hand rested on it, forefinger tapping against the polymer of the holster. "BramCo Mineral Acquisitions Security Police" was stenciled onto his body armor along with what looked like sergeant's stripes, but there was no name tag to go with it.

Dog whined slightly, as if he was insulted not to be included in the question, but I silenced him with a nudge of my toe.

"I'm Grant Masterson," I said, offering the man a hand. He ignored it and I shrugged, withdrawing both the hand and any good will I might have extended along with it. "I'm the owner and pilot of the *Charietto*." I motioned towards Beckett. "This is my apprentice, Rebecca Mitchell."

"What the hell kind of name is that for a ship, anyway?" That wasn't Neanderthal, it was one of his subordinates, a skinny fellow nearly two meters tall, who I guessed had been raised on a lower-gravity world. Neanderthal glared at him for talking out of turn, but I went ahead and answered the question, anyway.

"Charietto was a bounty hunter," I explained. "One of the first. He was a German who worked for the Romans back around the 4th Century on Earth. Barbarians kept crossing the Rhine river to raid the local towns, so Charietto got a bunch of his friends together and hunted them down, killed them, cut off their heads and took them back to the Romans for the reward."

The thin man stared at me wide-eyed, as if the story had horrified him, but didn't risk another disapproving glare from Neanderthal for talking again.

"Our scans confirm your damage," Neanderthal said curtly. He still hadn't offered a name, so I was just going to keep thinking of him as Neanderthal until he did. "They also show it looks like blaster fire caused it. Who shot at you? Was it the Navy?"

"The Navy wouldn't have any reason to shoot at us," I assured him. "It was raiders. We tried to call the Navy for help, actually, but I got spooked when they damaged us and jumped away to the closest preprogrammed route I had in navigation, which was here."

Neanderthal grunted with obvious skepticism, and the sound seemed to go well with his looks.

"Is that a dog?" he asked, staring at Dog.

No, genius, it's an aardvark.

"He's a robot. Basic K-9 apprehension unit," I expounded. "He's programmed to restrain without harming and obey a few simple commands."

Except shut up. He never obeyed that one.

Neanderthal seemed to consider it all, trying to wrap his brain around our story and the facts he knew and come up with something sufficiently officious and paranoid without actually breaking the laws about helping damaged ships affect repairs.

"This is what's going to happen," he declared, finally. "You're all coming into the base and you're going to stay in one of the public areas where we allow visitors. If you have any weapons, you're to leave them here. No personal weapons are allowed in the facility. Our techs will board your ship and see if we can repair the damage to your drive. If we can't, we'll give you enough fuel and food to reach the next public station in the belt."

I shaped a silent whistle.

"That'd be like a forty-day trip one-way with the sublight engines," I calculated. I tried to put a little desperation into my voice. "I sure hope you can fix the hyperdrive."

"That's not my job," Neanderthal said without much sympathy. He motioned back at the lock. "Get inside. You'll be scanned before you're allowed out of the docking area, so don't try sneaking any contraband in with you." He turned to the tall man. "Officer Pruitt, you stay here and wait for the techs. I'll take Jones with me and escort the…guests inside."

He'd been about to say "prisoners," I'd have been willing to bet.

"Right, sure thing." Pruitt offered Neanderthal a casual salute, earning yet another dirty look.

The guy just couldn't win.

———

The public area reminded me a lot of the terminal of a commercial spaceport: uncomfortable furniture, boring entertainment programs running on a loop in the buggy, poorly-maintained holographic displays, and overpriced soy products masquerading as food in the vending machines. The only difference was, there weren't ten thousand other ill-tempered travelers waiting with us.

"Stay here," Neanderthal had told us, just in case we'd missed it the first time. "The doors require base ID to get through, so if you need anything, call security on the intercom." He'd pointed to a panel on the wall near the sealed hatch into the rest of the base. "There's food, water, bathrooms, everything you need in here. They'll call you when they figure out if your drive can be repaired, so don't bother us unless it's an emergency."

I'd rewarded him with a bland smile and an even blander reassurance.

"Don't worry, you won't even know we're here."

And I hoped I hadn't been lying to him.

"Dog, we close?"

Dog had his front paws draped over the public data terminal, looking for all the world as if he were about to start humping it. He had to establish a physical link to the terminal because a wireless connection would have been more easily detected…at least, that's what he always told me. What I know about cracking computer encryption could fit in the operating system for an electric toothbrush.

"Closer if you stop distracting me."

Which was a lie. He could talk just fine while penetrating a network. He just liked making me wait.

"Isn't someone going to notice this?" Beckett asked, glancing around nervously as if she could find the security cameras hidden in the walls or ceiling.

"Notice what?" I wondered. "A robot dog acting like a real dog? It's how most of them are programmed."

"I wouldn't know, I could never afford a robot pet. When I was a kid in Absolution, we had real pets. A German shepherd and a tomcat. Why the hell do people want robot dogs?"

"Places like the Panicle and the Paragon, space colonies, the taxes and quarantine fees for importing live animals make them too expensive for most people." I explained, trying very hard not to sound condescending. Not everyone had the same life experience I did. "Robots are cheaper and they don't carry diseases, or shed, or poop on the floor."

"Unless you piss us off," Dog added. "Put your 'link on the data terminal, meatsack."

He was speaking in a low enough tone that anyone listening on a security monitor would have trouble telling his voice from ours, but I still winced, feeling paranoid. I put my 'link on the flat, glowing data terminal, which would automatically charge it as well as letting it update its settings. A red light began flashing on the display screen, indicating it was receiving an update, then turned green with completion. Dog sat back down on his haunches with a look of self-satisfaction.

"Now you have clearance anywhere on Hanuman these rent-a-cop wannabes do," he told me. I picked up the 'link, staring at it for a second as if I could tell the difference. "Also," Dog added, "I fed their security cameras a simulated video loop I put together showing the two of you sitting around, going to the head, etc...."

He cocked an ear. "They'll figure it out eventually, but it should give us a couple hours."

"Then let's not waste it." I headed for the door, waving at the two of them to follow.

I had done dumber things in my life, of that I was sure. But at the moment, I just couldn't think of one.

[9]

THE HATCH to the restricted sections of the base was thick and imposing, grey metal with officious warnings plastered across it telling us the penalties for unauthorized entry. I held my 'link up to the ID plate mounted on the wall beside it and waited, wondering if today would finally be the day Dog screwed up. A heavy, scraping clank from a metal bolt sliding out of its housing answered with a resounding "no." I replaced the 'link on its belt clip and nodded at Dog before I grabbed the handle and pulled the door open. I wasn't armed and hadn't wanted to take the chance they'd have good enough scanners to pick up a blaster in Dog's hidden compartment, so he was the best weapon we had right now. Though I wouldn't have admitted it to him.

The passage on the other side of the door was dimly lit and unoccupied, for which I murmured profound thanks to a God I hadn't spoken to much the last couple years. I wouldn't have put it past Neanderthal to leave a guard outside the door, but maybe he figured it was a waste of personnel. I knew they couldn't have too many security guards here—the expense of housing and feeding them would have been hard to justify to corporate. Maybe ten or twelve, tops, I figured, and half those off-shift at the moment.

The tunnel went down about thirty meters before it split in two. I shot Dog a questioning look and he sighed his exasperation and led us off to the left.

"It's on your damned 'link," he told me as he passed by.

"And maybe I don't want to be caught staring at my 'link if trouble pops up."

"Do you two always argue like this?" Beckett asked me. I'd been a bit worried about her rabbiting on us, but she was sticking to me like a covalent bond and she nearly ran into me when I paused to turn back to her.

"You can back up just a little, Ms. Beckett," I said, cocking an eyebrow. "I promise I ain't gonna run off and leave you."

"Sorry." She held back a step as I kept walking, following Dog, who hadn't stopped and was casting an annoyed glance back at us.

"And to answer your question, yes, we always argue just like this. Dog says it's an inevitable result of him being forced into subservience to an inferior intellect. I personally think he's just bored."

"Why not both?" Dog suggested.

The corridor wound further to the left and took us to a ramp heading downward. Stairs weren't necessary in the low gravity here and ramps were much easier to build. Dog scampered down the thirty-degree slope easily while the two of us followed at a more sedate pace. Falling would hurt less here, too, but I didn't want to put the physics to the test personally.

There were hatchways set on either side of the passage, some of them little more than cheap, plastic doors plainly marked as storage closets or bathrooms while others were airlocks connected to other cylindrical corridors leading to the other domes. Dog ignored them all, so I did too, except for a longing look at the bathroom. I should have gone before we left the ship. I'd barely had the thought when Dog sprinted to his right, straight for one of the storage rooms.

He didn't say anything, for once, and he didn't have to. His hearing was better than ours and if he was heading for cover, it meant someone was coming. I lunged ahead of him and pulled at the door handle, finding it unlocked. Inside was darkness and the musty stench of dust and old chemicals, but I pushed Beckett ahead of me and shut the door, knowing nothing we'd inside was worse than being found outside. Beckett moved behind me and I heard her bump into something metal and send it scraping across the floor.

Dog shushed her urgently but I just put a hand on her arm, squeezing gently in what I hoped was reassurance. Yelling at someone close to panic isn't the best way to calm them down in my experience, but Dog wasn't as much of a people person as I was. If he was a person at all. We'd had long debates about that, but if the Union courts still couldn't decide, I doubt the two of us were going to be able to hash it out.

It was pitch-black in the closet, just the barest slice of dim light creeping under the bottom of the door, and only Dog's teeth and eyes showed in the dark…and a flickering shadow from the hallway outside. Boot soles scraped on concrete floor and the tones of casual conversation filtered through the door, muted and incomprehensible. I figured Dog could probably hear them and I caught his attention with a motion.

"Do you think they know we're here?" I asked, too softly for even Beckett to pick up from a few centimeters away, much less anyone out in the corridor. But I knew Dog would hear.

He shook his head, the movement just barely visible. He couldn't tell me anything else, but that was enough. I made myself relax just a bit, despite chafing at the wasted time. There was still the whole part where we had to get back before they figured out we were gone. I waited until the footsteps had faded and the shadows were past, and reached for the door handle, but I felt Dog's teeth bite down ever-so-gently into my calf, just a slight jab through the tough cloth of my pants, and I paused.

He let go and moved up against the door, his body blocking out the light. I gave it another few seconds, letting him use his enhanced hearing to make sure the passers-by had really passed by, and finally he stepped back.

"Go," he said. "Hurry, before some other malingering meat-sack wanders through here."

He didn't wait for us once the door opened, just trotted away and left it to Beckett and me to keep up. I wanted to sprint after him, but I didn't know if Beckett was a runner, and I figured she'd spent the last year or so driving a truck and visiting the bar every night, which didn't exactly encourage physical fitness. I kept my pace to a brisk jog and she managed to hang with me, though her heavy, whooshing breaths nearly drowned out the smack of her soles on the floor, every step an echoing impact that made me wince in sympathy.

I wondered how long she could keep it up, and I was about ready to ask Dog to slow down when he turned right into a connecting hallway and came to an abrupt halt in front of a hatchway indistinguishable from any of the others except for a small label affixed to the thick, metal door with a stylized nautilus shell. Beckett stumbled from a quick jog to a walk, then skidded to a stop next to me and I checked behind her reflexively, making sure no one was following.

No one was there, but I still felt an itch between my shoulder blades. Dog had taken care of the security cameras in the waiting area, but there were still more along the corridors. The only advantage we had was that no one would be looking for us on them since they thought they knew where we were. Any of the guards monitoring the cameras could see anywhere in the base, most likely, but they didn't have enough people to see everywhere at once.

The door into the Nautilus dome was sealed with an ID plate and I pulled my 'link again, ready to use it to open the lock, but Dog shook his head.

"Won't work," he told me. "This place isn't run by the mining corporation. It's on its own separate security system. Give me a second."

He put his forepaws up against the wall, trying to reach the pad…and came up several centimeters short. He actually hesitated a moment before glancing back at me with what looked suspiciously like a wounded expression, the sort a real dog might give you when it's peed on the floor and knows it screwed up.

"I'm gonna need a hand here, Masterson."

I very carefully did *not* smile or laugh, knowing the inevitable argument that would ensue and also knowing we didn't have the time for it. I just came up behind him and wrapped my arms around his waist, lifting him up using my legs and not my back— he was a lot heavier than he looked.

"I know you're just loving this," he said.

"Just get it done," I urged him, already starting to feel a bit of strain.

His head was right in my face and I spit fur out of my mouth, wishing I could see what he was doing. Not that I would have understood it even if I could have seen it, but anything would have been better than a thirty-second deadlift of a seventy-kilogram robot. A far-away click signaled that something had happened, but Dog remained silent, eyes still fixed on the ID plate, fur still trying to work its way into my mouth.

"Any time now," I grunted, a muscle fluttering in my core.

"If you want them to seal us in here, or bust in and arrest us, then you can put me down now. Otherwise, I'm going to need another few seconds to penetrate the Nautilus security protocols."

Beckett was beside me and I felt her arms wrapping around dog beneath mine, taking some of the weight off me. I sighed just a bit in relief and nodded my thanks.

"That's done it," Dog announced almost immediately, making me suspicious he'd just been forcing me to hold him up for the sheer fun of it. "You can use the manual hatch release."

I dropped him none too gently, his claws scratching against the hard floor as he fought to retain his balance, and grabbed the release lever with both hands, yanking downward. The smell of must and disuse wafted out from the other side, and a darkness broken only by the frosted glow of emergency strip lighting. Past the entrance hallway was a huge storage room, the ceiling climbing higher, almost to the exterior shielding of the dome, a dusty, vacant cathedral completely empty.

A broad cargo airlock at least five meters across took up one wall, and I would have been willing to bet the dome was connected to its own landing platform to unload freight without any prying eyes watching. A utility locker was built into the wall next to the airlock, all the doors hanging open, the space within empty, except for one at the very end. I pulled at the handle and it stuck, but a more determined yank on it wrenched it free. Instead of the treasure trove of proof I'd been looking for, I was gifted with three ratty, faded space suits.

"Shit," Beckett hissed from behind me. I glanced back and saw her staring at the emptiness with an expression of almost devastation, as if she'd expected there to be incontrovertible proof sitting there on the floor for us to find.

"Pull the hatch shut," I told her.

Dog was pacing around the storage area, sniffing in a very dog-like way, running the dust and detritus through chemical sensors, spectrometers and a half a dozen other tests I wasn't smart enough to understand even if he'd taken the time to explain them. I let him go about his business, walking past the cargo bay and through the open doorway into what looked like it had once been a break room. The furniture was gone, but I could see marks on the counter where an auto-kitchen had sat, and maybe a refrigerator. There were cabinets built into the walls above the counter, as empty as the cargo bay now, but once they'd held king-sized containers of soy paste and spirulina powder. No steak and potatoes on an airless moon unless you were rich enough to afford a lab to grow it yourself.

A single, broad corridor led past the break room to employee housing, a few dozen tiny, single-bed apartments barely larger than my cabin aboard the *Charietto*. The beds remained, stripped to bare metal, but the walls were bare. I suppressed a policeman's urge to search the drawers of the nightstands and dressers, knowing there wasn't time, and moved on through to what had to be some sort of lab. It had once been sealed off, but the airtight pressure lock hung open now, as abandoned and unused as the rest of the place.

Stencils on the Spartan, grey walls provided dire warnings about contamination from untreated air and how anyone coming in through the lock must wear cleanroom suits and surgical masks or face immediate termination. I assumed they meant they'd fire the offending party, but given what I knew of their practices, murder might not have been out of the question. The interior was darker than the rest of the place, lacking even the emergency lighting. I didn't want to search around for a switch, so I pulled a flashlight off my belt and shined it around the room.

It was big, forty meters square I estimated, the walls and floors all the same stark, sterile white. All that was left of the lab was a double row of what looked like hospital beds with attachment points built into the side rails for some sort of monitoring equipment.

"What were they doing with those?" Beckett asked, pointing at the beds.

"Human experimentation," I guessed. "Just the sort of thing you'd come to an isolated mining colony to pull off without Union oversight."

"Whatever they were doing," Dog added, padding into the chamber behind us, "they had a shitload of Bartoli crystals here. I can still pick up the residual radiation signature."

"There's nothing left, though," Beckett declared, a hopeless moan below the words. "They stripped it all clean."

"Maybe not everything," Dog said.

Without elaborating, he moved down the length of the room, head swinging back and forth, ears pricked up, nose in the air. None of that was strictly necessary for his various scanners to work, and I had to think whoever had done his initial programming had quite the sense of humor.

Finally, almost to the opposite wall, he stopped and turned right, making a beeline to a spot just behind the last of the hospital beds. There was a metal platform there, wheeled at the base, with outlets built into the top, like something that might have been use to recharge portable equipment. Dog pulled open a small compartment at the base of the platform, hooking his claws into it and prying downward. Curious, I stepped up and shined my flashlight into the panel he'd opened, catching just a glimpse past his head of various physical data inputs.

"What is it?" Beckett asked. I was glad she'd asked instead of me, because he probably would have let me stew on it.

"Humans forget things," Dog declared. "I don't have that problem, but it comes in handy sometimes. Like charging stands. They charge instruments but they also have automatic data backup. It only lasts until the next user plugs in, but if no one has used this stand since Nautilus did whatever they were doing here..."

"Thank God for redundancy," I said, shaking my head. It was

about time inefficiency and bureaucratic screw-ups worked in my favor.

God didn't respond and neither did Dog. His face was buried in the compartment and I caught a glint of light off metal where something jagged and unnatural was extending from his left eye to plug into the physical connection. The hairs on the back of my neck stood up at the unwelcome reminder of exactly what Dog was. Sure, I repeated "he's a robot" so many times I could practically hang a sign around my neck, but it was easy to forget, not that he wasn't a dog but that he wasn't a biological entity at all. I was beginning to understand why sentient AI were so strictly regulated. It wasn't the harm they'd do to us, it was how the general public might start to feel about them.

"Okay, there's a shitload of data here," he announced after a few seconds. "I'm just skimming the interesting parts while I download it, but there were definitely human subjects present. No names, just randomly-generated number designators, but there's a personal history giving their medical backgrounds..." He trailed off, which meant he'd found something he needed to concentrate on. "That's funny. Same thing in common for every single one of the subjects."

"They all got paid?" I couldn't keep the cynicism out of my tone, I'm afraid.

"Funny, meatsack. No, they're all pilots. Mostly ex-Navy, some commercial, but they all have over 10,000 hours in hyperspace. Noted in their files in each case."

"Why is that important?" Beckett wondered. She'd crept closer until she was up even with me, and I could see the look of almost disgust on her face at the computer connection extending from Dog's eye.

"Don't ask me, honey, ask Nautilus," Dog replied. "There." The connector withdrew back into his head and the eye slipped back into place as if it had never left. He turned back to us, grinning, suddenly very dog-like again. "Got it all. We can review it at our leisure, so I suggest we haul ass back to the holding area before they figure out what we've been up to."

"You don't think there's anything else here we could use?" Beckett wondered, looking around as if some magic piece of evidence was going to drop out of the ceiling. "Will that data be enough?"

"It had better be," Dog snapped. "Because it's all we're getting out of this place."

"We need to go," I interjected, touching Beckett on the arm. "God knows how long we have before someone comes back to physically check on us in the…"

The alarm was a tiny, hollow whooping, the sound muted by the distance. I figured it didn't come over the speakers in the Nautilus dome because it was marked as unoccupied, but it filtered in from the hallway even past the closed hatch. It *could* have been anything, of course: an air leak, a drill, some sort of industrial accident… But it wasn't, and we all knew it.

"What now, fearless leader?" Dog asked me. He was being snarky, but the question felt honest. He might have been a super-computer, but he didn't know what to do, either.

"Let's get out of here and try to make it back as close as we can to the public area," I ventured, trying to smooth the ragged thoughts streaming through my head. "These guys might be pissed off at us, but they're just security guards, basically. They aren't going to shoot us if we're wandering around bored in the local company store, for instance."

"We're just going to throw ourselves on the mercy of the court?" Dog asked. "That's your plan?"

"If you come up with a better one between now and then, you let me know," I shot back over my shoulder, heading for the door.

Beckett had closed it, as I'd instructed, but it wasn't locked and it swung open toward me when I tugged on the handle. I poked my head out carefully, seeing nothing out to the end of the side corridor that had led down here from the main hallway, and I waved the others to follow. I jogged to the next junction, trying to get as much distance between us and the Nautilus lab as possible. The farther we got without running into anyone, the better I was feeling about the plan. Dog was tucked in behind me, trying to keep out of sight, while Beckett was huffing and puffing, just keeping up on my left side.

The klaxons were louder out here, their blaring hoots grating at my nerves, but I tried to make my pace deliberate and not panicked. There were people out here in the main corridor now, not security guards but regular workers here at the station, technicians and repair specialists in unremarkable, grey work clothes emblazoned with corporate logos. They weren't looking at us, simply staring up at the speakers where the klaxons originated, trying to read the flashing marquis floating by on message strips on the upper corner of the main hall.

It was saying something about intruders, giving a description and pictures of us. I ducked my head down and walked past the workers, hoping they'd be so wrapped up in reading the scroll that they wouldn't notice what we looked like. It almost worked.

"Hey!" The man's voice was loud and obnoxious, pitched high enough to carry over even the alarm. "Is that a fucking dog?"

"No, it's a robot," I hissed under my breath. "Go!"

We ran. It probably wasn't the smartest thing in the world, but I wasn't feeling particularly smart at the moment. This whole enterprise had been seat-of-the-pants and I shouldn't have been surprised when it fell to pieces. I had resigned myself to the idea that we were all going to be spending at least a few days in the local lock-up, so when I saw a squad of security guards coming around the corner, pushing through a small crowd of workers, I just slowed to a walk, motioning for Dog and Beckett to do the same.

Beckett looked grateful for the break, her face red, sweat matting her hair, while Dog seemed annoyed.

"I can take them out before they know what happened," he offered, and I knew it wasn't an idle boast.

"Yes, because then we can explain to the Marshals why exactly we committed a federal crime in the process of trespassing on corporate property." I raised my hands by my side in a calming gesture as the guards saw us and began steering through the small crowd of workers toward our position. "Everyone just stay calm and keep your mouths shut."

Especially you, Dog, I thought at him but refrained from saying. No use getting him more riled up.

As the guards approached within thirty meters, I saw they were led by Neanderthal himself, and he didn't look happy. Nor, I noted with a bit of concern, did he exactly look angry, not the way he had before. Instead, his broad, heavy-boned face seemed set in fearsome determination…and his hands were filled with the ugly, utilitarian lines of a blaster carbine.

"Hey, man, I'm really sorry," I said, pitching my voice to carry over the blare of the alarms. "We got kind of restless and the door just opened up for us, so…"

Fire exploded from the muzzle of Neanderthal's blaster and I was falling…

[10]

It took my brain a few seconds to process exactly what had happened. Something had yanked hard on the tail of my jacket and I was flying backwards, the fall seeming to take forever, and before my back even hit the floor, something hot and blinding was passing through the space where I'd been a half-second before. Time snapped back like a broken rubber band on impact, the cold concrete and the contrasting heat of the blaster fire just over my head bringing me to reality.

They were shooting at us. It seemed like an overreaction, but I wasn't going to stick around and try to argue them out of it. Dog had pulled me down, his senses and reaction time better than any human's, and now he yanked me up, grabbing my left sleeve and tugging me forward, his claws scratching against the floor for purchase. Beckett was staring in disbelief, the proverbial deer in the headlights, until I crashed into her, my chest ramming against her shoulder and carrying her along back the way we'd come.

People were screaming and scattering, already panicked by the alarm and now pushed over the brink by the gunfire, and their chaos kept us alive a few seconds longer than we had any right to expect. Not even Neanderthal and his goons were willing to fire into their own workers to get to us, which was more ethics than I'd given them credit for, but the respite was going to be brief.

"Where are we going?" Beckett asked, her voice high-pitched and tinged with panic.

I made a split-second decision, my subconscious processing data I didn't even remember knowing.

"Back to the Nautilus lab!" I said. "Stay close to the right-hand wall!"

The workers running away from the gunfire were mostly keeping to the right side of the corridor, a natural herd reaction to danger and one I was going to do my best to take advantage of. We weaved through the clusters of workers and a face here and there struck me: a middle-aged man with a grey-streaked beard and cheeks ruddy with exertion; a woman so young I might have justifiably called her a girl, with her blond hair tied into a ponytail and her eyes wide with abject fear.

A flare of blaster fire spalled burning concrete off the wall just above our heads and someone screamed. Guilt stung hard in my chest, because I was the cause of the fear, the reason they were in danger, and I would have given myself up if it had been an option, but summary execution didn't appeal to me. I felt a mixture of relief and fear when the civilians began to turn off from the main corridor ahead of us, heading somewhere I guess they considered safe and leaving us with no cover.

"Faster!" I urged Beckett. I wanted to grab her and pull her along, but it was an irrational impulse and would have just thrown us both off balance and slowed us down. But we were running as fast as she could and I could feel the sights settling onto my back and the finger tightening on the trigger.

Dog surprised me. He does that now and again, acts like maybe he cares whether I live or die. The move was so fast I barely followed it, as graceful as the pounce of a leopard onto a gazelle. One moment he was galloping a few meters ahead of me and the next he was using his momentum to climb up the side of the right-hand wall, then bounding off of it to the left, ricocheting off the opposite side and back into the pack of guards behind us.

He didn't do as much damage as he could have. He could have killed every single one of them, ripped their throats out or sliced through their femoral arteries. Instead, he just slammed into Neanderthal with a cross between a body block and a hip check, sending the big man tumbling forward, tripping up the two guards following close behind him in a chain-reaction like bowling pins going down. My head whipped around as I tried to follow the brown blur of Dog's trajectory, and I nearly tripped over my own feet when he bounded away from Neanderthal and dashed back ahead in a flurry of scraping claws.

The delay was just enough, and no gunfire followed us when we turned the corner into the side hallway to the Nautilus lab.

"What the hell?" Beckett demanded, pushing the door shut. This time I made sure to lock it behind us and she collapsed against it as I did, holding her head in her hands, hyperventilating. "Why did they start shooting at us?"

"Yeah, I might have some idea about that," Dog said. "I was going through the records I skimmed from the memory download. You know that company that hired the guards, BramCo Mineral Acquisitions Security Police? Three guesses who their parent corporation is, and the first two don't count."

"Nautilus," I hissed. "They're not just rent-a-cops, they're hired guns."

"And we just handed ourselves over to them," Beckett moaned.

"This was your idea," I reminded Dog.

"And coming back here and shutting ourselves in was yours," he shot back. "Did you have a plan beyond run and hide?"

"Run and hide is a good plan," I insisted. "But yes. We're going back to the *Charietto* and getting off this damned rock."

"How are we gonna do that with all those guards ready to shoot us the minute we set foot out in the hallway?" Beckett asked, staring at me with disbelief in her eyes.

I nodded toward the locker I'd left hanging open with the spacesuits still hanging from their racks.

"We're going to take an alternate route."

"I think we're about even in the dumb-ass idea category now," Dog said, his voice small and tinny over the helmet radio of the battered, old spacesuit.

I wasn't sure if I could disagree. Going outside through the Nautilus airlock had sure *seemed* like a great plan, and the fact that the suit tanks had been charged with air and their systems were both still working had been a real stroke of luck. Until we'd gone out the lock and realized the landing platform for the dome was still nearly a hundred meters above the surface of the planet.

I'd felt very much like a bug on a plate standing out there on the circular platform, three hundred meters across and perfectly flat, an island of grey metal on a dull, yellow plain of sulfurous hell. Above us, Agni stared down balefully, its yellow and orange and red clouds seething with rage at the intrusion into this, the realm of ancient gods. Around us, rising high above the angry, volcanic surface, were the domes. They'd seemed tiny and claustrophobic from the air, but down among them, they were huge, man-made mountains.

"Should we try to climb along the outside?" Beckett had asked. Her tone was a bit shrill and I wondered if she'd ever been outside on a hostile world in nothing but a suit. It was a humbling experience. "There're probably maintenance catwalks on the exterior of the domes."

"Monitored, certainly," Dog had nixed the idea with a shake of his head. It was incongruous seeing him out there in the thin, poisonous air, as if he were some phantom haunting the installation, a ghost dog from another time. "The only way to get through to the landing platform where they have our ship is on the ground, at the base of the domes. Too much area down there for anyone to watch it all."

Another idea which had made sense, until we'd found out the only way down from the outside of the landing platform was a narrow, rickety ladder attached to the skin of the support column. Which ladder we would have to descend in spacesuits where you couldn't see your feet to know if you were about to miss a rung. Oh, and did I mention Dog wasn't built to go down ladders? Up, sure, no problem. Down, not so much.

So, there I was, 250 meters over jagged, unforgiving lava rock, trying to climb down a ladder one-handed, unable to see my feet or feel a thing through the thick, protective boots, while carrying a 120-kilo robot dog under one arm. The weight wasn't that bad, given the gravity on the moon was a third standard, but even at a third of his normal weight, Dog was an armful, and 300 meters was a long climb.

I felt hampered by my resolve not to curse, because I surely wanted to. Fatigue was straining both forearms and my shoulders were on fire, tense from the load and equally as tense because I was just plain scared. I hadn't let on to Beckett because she was nervous enough for all three of us, but I didn't much care for spacesuits. The hard, outer surface, armored against impacts and radiation, constricted my chest and made it hard to draw a full breath. The faceplate only exacerbated the feeling, reflecting just a bit of carbon dioxide back into me with each exhalation, until my hindbrain became convinced that I was about to asphyxiate despite the fact I was getting plenty of air. The intellectual part of my mind knew that, anyway.

Dog could probably read my heartrate and blood pressure even through the suit, so he wouldn't be fooled by my brave act, but I kept it up, just the same. No use giving him more ammunition.

"What happens if they spot us on the ladder?" Beckett asked. "Do we have a backup plan?"

"That would be Plan C," Dog told her, deadpan. "We're already on Plan B. You don't really want to know what Plan C is."

"If anything happens," I cut in, trying to keep her calm, "just follow me and try to keep behind cover. Everything will be all right."

The bottom edge of the domes passed by and we were climbing down the side of one of the ten-meter-wide shock absorbers they rested on, keeping them stable through the tectonic travails of the moon. I tried to concentrate on the intricate details of the supports, losing myself in the ragged network of abrasions cut into the metal surface from years of exposure to caustic chemicals. When my foot touched ground, it surprised me enough I nearly cried out and made myself look like an idiot. I was so relieved to set Dog down, I wouldn't have cared.

"Thank God," he said, hopping out of my arms before I had the chance to lower him to the sandy, rock-strewn surface. "If I never have to be carried by a human again, I will die a happy robot."

I took a moment to catch my breath and work out the cramps in my arms and quadriceps, leaning forward and trying to get a sense of our surroundings now that I could see again. Everything seemed so much bigger down here, closer. The colors were brighter, the rocks sharper and more jagged, the clouds of sulphur dioxide a white haze drifting across the face of the gas giant.

Shadows stretched out around us, the looming menace of the domes casting a pall over the harsh, unforgiving environment.

It seemed like an excellent place to get ourselves killed.

"Dog, take point," I said. "Delia, you're in the middle and I'll bring up the rear."

How much good I'd do unarmed and in a space suit, I wasn't sure, but it was the tactically sound decision. And I had to let Dog walk point because I sure didn't know which way we should be going. Beckett didn't complain and, for once, neither did Dog. He did start bounding off without us at way too fast a pace, taking for granted we could adapt to the low-gravity hop as easily as he could. And honestly, I could have, but Beckett wasn't nearly as experienced in different gravity fields and looked as if she were trying to ice-skate in dirt.

"Slow it down a bit, partner," I cautioned. "Not everyone's got computer-controlled gyros."

"I can go just as slow as you meatsacks want. It's your lives, after all."

I was sure that would make Beckett feel all sorts of better. I knew it cheered me right the heck up.

"I can go a little faster," Beckett insisted. She experimented with a bunny-hop, both legs at once, but it was awkward and slow.

"Just a giant step," I advised her. *One small step for a man*, a voice from a long-ago history class whispered in my ear, *one giant leap for mankind*. Right then, I would have been satisfied with a few medium-sized steps for these particular humans.

She tried it, a tentative bound at first, then fell into a sustainable rhythm and I followed behind. It was about ten times as difficult trying to keep up the pace while checking our six o'clock every second step, all in a space suit. I couldn't turn my head, so I had to turn my whole body, 360 degrees in mid-air and it was making me dizzy after about the first hundred meters. I could tell right away that wasn't going to be sustainable and cut it back to one rearward glance every sixth or seventh step.

That's probably how they were able to sneak up behind us. One step, one turn to check behind us and we were clear, nothing but the fearsome vistas of Hanuman and the Brobdingnagian expanse of the domes and the equipment supporting them. The next, just twenty or thirty seconds later, and they were just there. I might not have seen them at all if it hadn't been for the flare of an outgassing reflecting off a spacesuit visor, but the glint revealed them as surely as a spotlight. There were four of them, scuttling cockroaches beneath the floorboards, a hundred meters behind us and moving up fast, much faster than I thought we could manage with Delia slowing us down.

My reaction was instinctive, less a plan than an adrenalin spike. Flight was out, so fight it was.

"Behind us!"

I didn't remember making the decision to shout, heard the words as if they came from someone else, maybe the same person who was turning and bounding into a single, powerful leap just as high as muscles born on Earth and trained on planets with even higher gravity could take me. I was soaring upward, five meters off the ground, ten meters forward, the moon and the dome and everything on either side a blurred streak, while the glittering faceplates of suit helmets and the wicked, angular curve of blaster carbines came into preternaturally sharp focus.

I'd been trying to get their attention on me, away from the others, and it had worked a bit too well. Sizzling, crackling blaster fire passed only centimeters from my head, one bolt of scintillating energy actually burning through the space between my left arm and my side, leaving charred, blackened streaks on my suit. It seemed like I hung up in the air forever, a floating, reactive target to test the marksmanship of the station's hired guns. They needed practice.

I came down right in the middle of them and my shoulder slammed into a chest. I hadn't planned it that way and it really didn't work out how I would have hoped, because the chest plate of a spacesuit is pretty hard and unyielding. Pain wrenched through my arm and upper back, sharp and hot, and stars swam over my vision. I forced down the pain, blinked back the stars and made myself keep moving, hoping I hadn't done anything truly, monumentally stupid like getting my faceplate cracked.

I was staring almost nose-to-nose at the man who I'd heard called Pruitt, my helmet only centimeters away from his, my hand resting against his shoulder where I'd grabbed it to steady myself. His face was pale, beaded with sweat, his eyes wide with shock and indecision. The security guards couldn't fire with me right in the middle of them, but they wouldn't want to put their guns down and wrestle hand-to-hand, either, if they could help it, which gave me a few seconds of confusion in which to act, and I tried to take advantage of it.

I grabbed at the emitter housing of his blaster carbine and yanked toward me, knowing he'd clamp down and hold onto the thing for dear life. When the gun came towards me, so did he... and so did the external controls for his suit. My fist was armored with a spacesuit glove designed to work outside among sharp, jagged lava rock and I smashed it into his faceplate with all the force and leverage I could build up. The faceplate cracked. It didn't shatter, which would have probably killed him, not from the lack of air but from the poisonous clouds of sulphur dioxide, but the cracks were a spider-web spreading across the visor.

The man panicked. I'd seen in his eyes he would. He could have kept fighting, trusting in the construction of the suit to hold together until he got back inside, but instead, he let the blaster carbine go and ran, heading back to whatever access airlock they'd all come through in the first place.

I'd had seconds of advantage and it ran out about the same

time Pruitt did. The other three security thugs had finally figured out what was going on and they'd all reached their own conclusions about how to solve the problem. One of them was backpedaling with quick, urgent steps, giving himself room to aim his gun at me, while the other two grabbed at my arms and shoulders, trying to wrestle me to the ground. I had the blaster carbine, but I was holding it by the barrel and there was no way I was going to have time to flip it around or even use it as a club with the two guards weighing me down.

I was just about done. I was still struggling, still trying to break free and simultaneously keep the two security guards between me and the one with the gun pointed, but I knew winning one battle would lose me the other. Lucky for me, I wasn't alone. A brown blur slammed into one of the guards holding my arm, a torpedo of fake fur and real attitude. The man's grip jerked loose from my right arm and he tumbled backwards, head over heels, not stopping until he bounced off the side of one of the dome support columns.

The one who'd been holding onto my left arm had kept his helmet tucked against my shoulder, trying to keep me from getting to his faceplate, but when Dog attacked, his head snapped up and I saw the whites of his eyes, saw his lips skin back off his teeth in shock and sudden fear. I was cocking my arm back to take a swing at his helmet when he did exactly the right thing…or exactly the wrong thing, if you were looking at it from our perspective. He pushed away from me, blindly, desperately, just wanting to get distance between himself and Dog.

Dog knew what was going to happen and so did I. I fumbled with the blaster carbine, lunging forward to one knee just to keep in motion but knowing my only chance twas to be faster on the trigger than the other guy. Dog took another tack, rushing straight at the gunman, betting shock and surprise and his sheer speed would be enough to take the guy down before he could fire.

He was wrong. Star-white energy lanced outward and Dog twisted in mid-leap, trying with every bit of preternatural machine agility he had to avoid the burst of blaster fire. He couldn't quite do it. Sparks flashed and Dog slumped to the ground in a halo of smoke.

[11]

"Goddammit!"

I wasn't sure which surprised me the most, the curse that wrung its way free of my lips against my will, or the reflexive squeeze of my finger on the carbine's trigger pad. A blinding fusillade of actinic energy gushed from my carbine's emitter, a firehose of plasma that had to have drained the power pack. What was left of the gunman bore very little resemblance to a human being and was barely held together by what was left of the spacesuit.

Something nagged at the back of my mind, the conviction I was forgetting something, and I knew as quickly as the thought passed from one side of my brain to the other exactly what it was. The last guy had a gun, and just because he was panicked didn't mean he wasn't about to use it. My carbine was empty and I was in an awkward position, down on one knee. It would take a second for me to get into motion, and I had the sense it was a second I couldn't spare.

Beckett saved me. She was running clumsily, inexpertly in the low gravity, and she would have been an easy target if the last guy had even been looking at her, but he only had eyes for me. I threw myself to the side as he fired, feeling the scorching heat of his blast just before it cut off as Delia Beckett smashed a rock down on the side of his helmet.

It stunned him, enough to send his blaster carbine flying away, but she'd missed his faceplate and those helmets were meant to take punishment. And panicked or not, this guy was a professional. He swiped a hand backward at Beckett and she jerked away, her sharp cry a burst of static in my headphones, and it was only then I noticed the knife. The blade was short and curved and finished a matte black, almost invisible in the shadows below the domes.

My first instinct was to shoot him. Knives are no joke, even when you're not in a spacesuit, where any cut deep enough to penetrate at a key point can be fatal. You walk into a knife fight, one of you is going to the hospital and the other is probably going into the recyclers. I had no qualms at all about putting a round through someone threatening me with a knife, Marshal or not.

But my gun was empty, and Dog was down and I was fairly certain Beckett had a rip in her suit. I reversed the carbine in my hands, wielding it like a club, and waded into a knife fight like a huge idiot.

The guy was fast and he knew how to use that knife. He slashed at me with an upward flick of his wrist and the blade skittered off the blaster's emitter housing with a scrape of metal on metal that set my teeth on edge. I curled the butt of the gun around in a tight arc, not swinging it wildly to avoid telegraphing my shot, and felt the crack of connection. I'd had to aim carefully. His forearms and the backs of his gloves were armored just like mine, but there was a weak spot at the wrist—there had to be or else he wouldn't have been able to rotate his hands. It was a gasket, tough and resilient but not much of a cushion; when the buttstock hit, it struck the radial nerve. I knew that because the man's fingers opened up and the knife flew free.

I wasn't on the same radio frequency as the security guard, but I could see his lips moving through his faceplate, and I was pretty sure he was cursing in a stream-of-consciousness free flow, holding his wrist and letting his eyes dance around between me and Beckett…and his carbine, which was between the two of us, laying half-buried under a layer of volcanic dust.

I waited for him to make a reach for it, prepared to club him down with my empty gun, but Beckett moved first. She threw herself forward, digging the carbine out of the dirt and squeezing the trigger before she even had it pointed at him. White-hot energy beams sprayed wildly, none coming within a meter of the security guard, but that was enough for the man. He turned and ran, following the same path back as the first of them, barely ahead of the last burst of blaster fire Beckett sent chasing after him.

"That's enough," I told her, grabbing the barrel of the weapon to make sure she didn't accidentally shoot me. She let free of the gun and rolled over onto her side.

This close, I could see that her face had gone pale and I began searching for the rent in her suit. I knew there had to be one and I was hoping it wasn't somewhere vital. I found it easily, its surface scabbed over with frozen blood. She'd taken the cut to her elbow gasket and it was a ragged enough hole that the suit hadn't been able to automatically seal the way it was designed.

"Hold still," I cautioned her, reaching for the emergency repair kit every spacesuit was required by Union regulations to carry on its tool belt.

Hers was right where it was supposed to be and I yanked open the hard, polymer pouch and pulled out the sealed plastic bag. The applicator inside it was crude and single-use, basically a tube of fast-drying glue, but I had to hope it would get her back to the ship before it failed. I spread it liberally over the slice in her gasket, slathering it all the way around her elbow joint just to make sure I didn't miss anything.

"Don't try to bend your elbow," I warned, holding her arm out stiff. "I think it would be okay, but this stuff might get brittle and I don't want it to start cracking."

She nodded inside her helmet, the instinct of someone who didn't use spacesuits very much, and I patted her on the shoulder comfortingly before rising and forcing myself to go check on Dog. I didn't want to. I didn't want to see what was left of him. Charred fur and blackened, jagged metal were all that was visible from the shadows where he'd curled up.

Just like a real dog, going off somewhere to die alone.

Most of the damage was to his rear left side, the leg there almost blown off, but the beam had penetrated through, deep into his interior workings. Maybe into his isotope power pack, maybe even into his CPU. He didn't keep it in his head because that would be vulnerable. Instead, it was at the center of his chest, which *should* have protected it, but...

"Can you hear me?" I asked, hoping against hope he'd answer over my radio and tell me what a useless meatsack I was. "Dog?"

He didn't answer, but his head moved. Just a few centimeters, but his eyes flickered open and focused on me. He said nothing and I wasn't sure if that meant his radio was damaged or his higher mental functions were fried. The first was reparable. The second...well, if I got him to one of the very few, very restricted AI service centers open only to Union law enforcement and military, they *might* be able to swap out parts and get his brain functioning again, but this was AI we were talking about. The consciousness of a human or an AI is a transcendent property, dependent on quantum uncertainty and the butterfly effect.

It wouldn't be him anymore.

"Just hold on," I said, not knowing if he could hear me, or if he could understand me even if he did. "I'll get you out of here."

I scooped Dog up like a baby. He wasn't dead weight, but then he wouldn't be, not with mechanical joints. He felt like a bag of spare parts and my gut churned at the sensation of him.

"Can you run, Delia?" I asked, not looking back at her.

"I think so." Her voice was weak and winded, and I didn't trust her words but there just wasn't any choice. I couldn't carry both of them and reinforcements would be coming.

"Follow me, then. And if you can't keep up, say something, because I won't be looking back."

———

"This is bad."

Delia Beckett's voice was strained and breathless and I thought if I turned and looked at her, she'd probably look just as bad through her helmet. I didn't bother because there wasn't a thing I could do about it. Instead, I crouched behind the sensor beacon pod at the edge of the landing pad and directed my attention toward the *Charietto*.

At least, I consoled myself, they didn't have her surrounded. They didn't have enough people for that. This was a small outpost and they had to be looking for us inside and out, which only left three of them to guard the ship. Well, to guard the ship on the outside. I was sure they had someone covering the airlock umbilical from inside the docking bay. The three guards carried blaster carbines but they weren't patrolling. They didn't seem to have much of a concept of discipline in this group of chuckleheads, which would have been so much more advantageous if we had guns.

Instead of maintaining a perimeter around the landing platform, the three of them were clustered beside the main boarding ramp, which had been left open, probably to discourage us from trying to get on board from inside the base. Hard to sneak on board through the docking umbilical when the ship was filled with sulphur dioxide. Those were the two main entrances, the boarding ramp and the utility airlock, and both were covered. Let me rephrase that…those were the two entrances they *knew* about.

"Stay here," I told Beckett, then touched her shoulder and pointed to Dog. He was motionless, a brown lump of fur on the platform beside us. "When I signal, you bring Dog and haul ass. Can you do that?"

Now I did look at her and it was just as bad as I'd imagined. Her face was drawn and slightly green, her skin slick with a fine sheen of sweat. It had been a hard climb and I think she'd had a little sulphur dioxide leak into her suit before I'd slapped the patch on—not enough to do serious damage, but enough to make her feel sick. She'd toughed it out and made it up here, though, which had impressed me.

"I will get him on board," she insisted through clenched teeth. "I can't promise I'll be able to stand up after that."

"I think we're all going to need a nice long rest after this." I patted her arm, then ducked around the sensor pod and ran toward the ship.

It was a foolhardy thing to do. I knew it, knew deep in my gut the odds were about even that one of them would turn around at just the wrong time, or someone inside would check a monitor and see me, and that would be that. There was nowhere to hide out here, just a hundred meters of open ground between me and the ship. I ran in a skating motion, trying to stay low to the ground, not wanting to risk a normal gait because the bounding step would have sent me meters into the air. It felt painfully slow, but in reality, I was eating up distance meters at a time in the low gravity, and it was only seconds before I was up against the port rear landing jack. I hugged it like a long-lost friend, taking a moment to catch my breath.

Just touching the ship made me feel less vulnerable, though

that was illusory, psychological. A nightmare vision of hell stretched all around us, and the grey metal of the dome seemed less a sanctuary from the outside than just a different sort of damnation, and the *Charietto* was the only shelter we had. If I could get into it…

There was a maintenance hatch under the delta wing just beside the landing jack. Normally, it would have been pressure-sealed off from the rest of the ship and there would have been no way to access the main cabin through it, but the ladies and gentlemen of BramCo had opened the boarding ramp and exposed the interior to the thin and poisonous atmosphere here on Hanuman. I pushed in an access panel two meters up in the underside of the wing and reached through to twist the lock for the hatch. It dropped open, swinging down like a pendulum, and would have kept its back-and-forth arc if I hadn't stopped it with a firm hand.

Darkness was inside the maintenance crawlway, a cramped, squared-off tunnel barely wide enough for a grown man to wiggle through it. The prospect of trying to squeeze into it, the possibility of getting stuck in there and being helpless, waiting to die, made my testicles crawl up inside my belly and weep. But there wasn't any other option. Surrender likely meant death, our bodies disposed of in some volcanic crater where no one would ever find them.

I jumped to get a hand-hold, then pulled myself up into the tunnel, kicking my legs behind me to push all the way inside. It was hard getting a full breath in the crawlway. Every time I tried, my shoulders pushed against the sides and I wanted to scream. I made my mind blank through an effort of will, picturing a beach, hot sand, the warmth of the primary star high above and the cool waves lapping against my legs. Slowly, my breathing came back under control.

I stretched my left arm out in front of me, tucked my right shoulder in and started moving forward. The edges of the spacesuit's environmental pack kept catching the top of the tunnel every time I scooted my lower body upward, and each time it did, I had to let the air out of my lungs and press my chest into the floor to get it free. Finally, I figured out I would need to pull myself forward a few centimeters at a time with my lead arm, pushing off with the side of my trailing foot. It was maddeningly slow and I longed for a full breath, for the opportunity to fill my lungs with air.

It's just ten meters. It's nothing. You could cross it in twelve big steps. Four or five in this gravity.

The lighter gravity was the only saving grace. If I'd been in standard gravity, I'd have been totally screwed, unable to breathe or move at all. As it was, I nearly missed my exit. I knew where it was, approximately, had seen it from the other side many times, but it was pitch black inside the crawlway and even if it hadn't been, my suit's faceplate was pressed up against the wall and I wouldn't have seen anything but dust and corrosion.

My lead hand missed the catch for the access panel and I couldn't even feel it through the suit's chest armor, but it happened to catch on the gasket over my right knee. I closed my eyes, hissing in frustration, and edged backwards. When my hand found the catch, I fumbled with it for a moment, unable to see it, trying to remember how to open it. I don't know what I did, but the panel gave way, swinging downward and taking me with it.

I bit back the cry of surprise trying to burst free as I fell through the hatch into the ship's utility bay, then went ahead and yelled because it was contained inside my helmet and no one would hear it but me. And God's honest truth, I was just so happy to be out of that crawlway I wanted to yell just for the sheer sake of it. With the low gravity, I didn't even bust my butt falling to the deck, just absorbed the landing with bent legs and steadied myself against a work bench.

The ship was dark and seemingly deserted, but I ran to the

weapons locker anyway, retrieving a blaster before I did anything else. Blasters are tools and I try not to get too sentimental about them, but I have to admit, it felt good having the gun in my hand right then. I checked behind me to make sure the guards hadn't come on board and snuck up on my six, then I ran to the cockpit.

I'd had long minutes inside the crawlway to think about this, and I probably needed a few minutes more because it wasn't a great plan, but it was all I had. At least it was simple. I hit the controls to warm up the reactor, which happened fairly silently and was hard to detect from the outside unless someone was watching through a thermal filter. It didn't take long, but I kept checking over my shoulder every two seconds, the blaster in my right hand aimed back behind me just to be sure.

When the indicators reached the green, I already had both hands poised over the command console and I hit the control to cut loose from the docking umbilical and fed power to the belly jets with two quick, stabbing motions. This was the tricky part. The guards outside would notice the turbines spinning up even in the thin atmosphere, and I couldn't close the belly ramp yet.

"Beckett!" I transmitted, scrambling out of the cockpit and back to the utility bay. "Now! Make for the ramp!"

I didn't wait for her reply. I had other things to worry about. Like my conscience. I knew the guards would try to come up the ramp to figure out what was going on once they noticed the jets warming up, and I knew I was a good enough shot to kill all three of them before they made it into the ship. But I didn't really want to kill anyone else. I'd killed one man today already, and I was fairly sure I hadn't had any choice in the matter, but that didn't mean I was free to just slaughter the rest of them indiscriminately.

For one thing, I wasn't a Union Marshal anymore and I only had the right to shoot someone in defense of myself or others. A jury might decide this was self-defense, since I was on board my own property and they were acting outside the law and could have been charged with false imprisonment, but I didn't really think this would ever come to trial, so that was a secondary consideration.

The main thing was, I didn't want to become a killer. I'd killed a few people in my day, a couple just a few days ago, but I wasn't a killer, wasn't someone who it came natural to. I had met men and women like that, had arrested them, had shot them down in the street, and had even worked with a few of them who'd manage to sublimate their killer instinct into something socially acceptable. Those Marshals who were natural killers weren't bad people, but they had to constantly struggle with their nature, constantly remind themselves who they were. I knew who I was and I didn't want it to change.

But I also had a responsibility to bring Beckett in alive, doubly so since I was the one who'd chosen to expose her to the danger here. I ducked behind a corner of the utility bay bulkhead, aimed my blaster and waited.

The first one up the ramp was running wildly, arms akimbo as if he expected some technical glitch rather than any real opposition, the look in his eyes that of a man who was deathly afraid he'd screwed up hard and had to fix it before anyone found out. I shot him in the left hip. An extremity shot would have been safest, but I wasn't confident enough to try one at that range, not with his arms and legs flailing about. I cringed as I saw him fold up, saw his mouth open in a scream inside his faceplate. The blaster bolt had probably broken his pelvis even through the armor of the spacesuit and I knew it had to hurt like a son of a gun on top of the emotional shock.

His carbine had been hanging loosely by the sling and he'd dropped it when he fell. I resisted an urge to go secure it because the others would be coming. They'd hear his scream and they'd be on their way before they understood his warning.

They came together, one right behind the other, which made it a harder shot. The one in front was a woman, or at least I thought so from her size and what I could see of her face through the helmet's visor. She had her carbine at her shoulder, carried at low-ready, much more on the ball than the first guy. I shot for the carbine and got her right shoulder. Light flashed from the vaporized armor and she went down as if she'd run into a wall.

She writhed on the floor, trying to get up to her knees, trying to reach for her gun, but I put another round into the carbine and hit the power pack this time. It blew in a halo of white light a meter across and she fell back again, hands going instinctively to her face and coming up short against her helmet's visor.

The second shot almost got me killed. The last of them was coming up just behind her and he saw me, saw the shot and knew exactly what was going on. He had his carbine to his shoulder, had me dead to rights and even as I swung my pistol toward him, I knew I wouldn't be in time.

Delia Beckett plowed into the man's back shoulder-first and his shot charred a black crater into the bulkhead instead of my face. The security guard stumbled forward off-balance, and Beckett tumbled to the deck beside him, Dog spilling out of her arms as she fell. I stepped out from behind the bulkhead, moving across the three meters separating us and grabbed the guard's carbine by the emitter housing, pulling him into a flat-footed kick to the chest.

He flopped backwards onto the ramp and kept falling, head over heels, unable to stop himself. I fired three quick shots off from my pistol into the landing platform surface at the end of the ramp, each hit producing a mushroom-cloud flare, and it was enough to send him running back for the airlock, probably trying to get help.

"Hurry!" I urged Beckett, grabbing the wounded and stunned female guard by the arm and dragging her toward the ramp.

She jerked against my hold, but the shoulder wound, and the

sulphur dioxide it had let seep into her suit before the automated repair systems had sealed the breach, were both working against her and her resistance was weak and ineffectual. I pushed her down the ramp and she went backwards off her feet, rolling down to the base and not trying to get up.

Beckett was coming up behind me, dragging the last of them by the shoulders. He was unconscious, probably put out by the suit's automated medical systems, and I could see the grey goo of the repair gel oozing out from the lining around the hole in his hip. He'd live, I told myself. They'd both live. At least I'd done my best to make sure they'd both live and that was all I could hope for under the circumstances.

The unconscious guard slid down the ramp on his back, then tumbled sideways when he hit the ground and came to a halt face down on the surface of the landing platform and didn't move. I hit the control to close the ramp and ran back to the cockpit.

"Strap in!" I warned Beckett, not bothering to fasten my own safety harness before I fed power to the jets.

The *Charietto* leapt into the sky on columns of fire, pushing me down into my seat, and I had never been quite so happy to be off the ground as I was at that particular moment. I slipped an arm through the seat restraints with desperate haste before hitting the main drives, hoping Beckett was smart enough to do the same. Boost pressed me backwards with merciless efficiency and the ship headed upward through the thin atmosphere at a steeper angle than she would have from a habitable world, nearly straight up.

I took a second to fasten my harness, then shut off the insistent, inane demands from the facility's traffic control, still threatening to turn me into the Marshals, the Navy and maybe the Boy Scouts if I didn't return immediately to the landing platform and surrender.

That would have been a whole lot more convincing if you

didn't keep trying to kill us, I thought at them. I could have broadcast it, but there was no use rubbing salt in the wound. Better they think we still didn't know what was going on.

The important thing was, they didn't have armed ships to chase after us…

"What's that?"

Beckett's voice startled me. Not that she was strapped into the copilot's position besides me, I'd expected that. It was just that hearing anyone except Dog talking to me during this sort of tense situation seemed wrong. I glanced over and saw she was pointing at a blip on the sensor screen, coming not from Hanuman surface or orbit but from a point just past the gravity well that could only mean the closest hyperspace jump distance.

That was an assumption, and I'd always had drummed into me as a cadet that when you assume, you make an ASS out of U and ME, but I felt like it was a justified one. Because this was the same ship that had attacked us over Morrigan, the same silvery delta shape right down to the scar of battle damage I'd left on her with our blaster cannons.

"Well," I murmured, "I suppose I should have expected this. Since when has everything not happened at exactly the wrong time?"

"Who is it?" Beckett asked and I remembered she wouldn't have any training in reading a ship's tactical display.

"Our old friends. Can you handle the blaster turret? Because I can't fly this thing and shoot both."

"I've never done it before," she admitted, as if it were something to be ashamed of.

"You see that bare spot on your right? The one that looks like there should be something there?"

"Yeah," she said after a minute. "That's where it is? The guns?"

"Reach underneath and flip up the panel."

She fumbled with it for a moment in silence and I wondered if I was going to have to go open it up for her when she barked triumphantly. The joystick and flat panel display swung upward into place and her hands hovered above it as if she were afraid she'd blow the ship up if she touched the wrong control.

"You see the big red button beside the joystick? Hit that to arm the turret."

I remembered she wouldn't have the codes, so I unlocked the controls from my station with a thumb on the ID panel.

"It turned on," she said, sounding excited, like that had been half the battle.

On the tactical display, the mercenary's ship was angling to intercept our course, trying to jump us when we broke orbit before we could reach minimum safe jump distance.

"When you twist the joystick around," I told her, trying to keep the words calm, trying really hard not to raise my voice, "it turns the whole turret and your view with it. It can be a bit like looking through a soda straw, so if you lose sight of the enemy ship, sneak a look up at the main screen and get an idea of our orientation, then try again."

"Okay," she said, eyes narrowed and focused on the targeting screen as she played with the joystick. "I think I get it."

"To fire, just push the trigger on top of the joystick with your thumb, but use short, quick bursts. You don't want to overheat the guns and crack our crystals. Got it?"

"I think so."

"I'll let you know when we're in range."

Which was going to be depressingly soon, given how fast both ships were moving. Man, I wished Dog were here. It felt strange flying into trouble without him in the cockpit. It felt way too much like being alone.

"I have the ship in the gun camera," Beckett told me. "It looks big. How long do I have to wait?"

Answering her question took longer than it should have. Dog would have been able to wrangle a calculation in a second, connected to the ship wirelessly through the link between his computer brain and the ship's. I had to scroll through a menu in the sensor display and try to tie it into the gun's software, which was a pain because the gun was a secret system and we didn't want to make it obvious we had it.

But finally...

"Thirteen seconds," I told her. "Ten." The fusion drive rumbled its vibration through the ship, the ride getting smoother as we left the vestiges of Hanuman's thin atmosphere. "Five."

Agni glowered at us as we left the realm of his children and entered his heavenly domain, meddlesome mortals, always bringing trouble with us.

"Three, two, one. Fire!"

They shot first. I could see the red flash of their blasters passing by us only meters away, still ablating shielding just from heat and radiation, sending a slight shudder through the ship at the outgassing of metal. A miss, but a near one, and I threw us into an evasion pattern, kicking the maneuvering jets this way, then that, starboard, up, down, port, just micro-adjustments to keep us in motion in their targeting screens.

"Delia?" I asked, looking over at her from the corner of my eye. "Any time now."

"Every time you move the ship, I lose target lock," she complained and I felt a vague irritation.

Was this how Dog felt around me all the time?

Another incoming burst, this one closer, and yellow warning lights flashed on the damage control display as it told me we'd just lost a centimeter of armor plating at the edge of our port wing. Nothing vital unless we had to land in an atmosphere, but I didn't like having bits blown off my ship, even if I wasn't using them at the moment.

"Just shoot at them, Delia," I told her. "Even if you don't have a solid lock, it'll keep them thinking about saving their own hides and less about ventilating ours."

"All right, all right," she said, clucking impatiently, her face locked in concentration.

We were three minutes from minimum safe jump distance, which seemed like an awful long time right at the moment.

Finally, she fired. I couldn't hear the actual discharge of course, probably wouldn't have seen anything if I'd been outside looking, but the computer simulated the energy pulses as stuttering red lines across the main display, connecting us with the silver delta of the enemy ship for a moment. It was still barely visible across the brooding face of Agni and the angry reds and yellows of Hanuman, but it cheered me up just a bit.

"I think you hit them!" I told her, trying to sound encouraging. At least, the thermal readings had showed a bloom on their portside near the bow, which could have been a hit. "Keep at it. Short bursts."

I was struck by a memory of teaching my son how to shoot at the police range, how his eyes had lit up the first time he'd hit the target with the training blaster. My gut clenched at the image and I wished for just a moment that the mercenaries would blow us out of the sky and put me out of my misery. I clenched my teeth and forced the feeling inward, locking it in that tight, cramped little space inside me where I kept all the hurt.

I worried, sometimes, what was going to happen when that space got too full and blew like an ancient steam boiler. I hoped whoever was on the receiving end deserved what they were going to get when it happened.

The *Charietto* shook like God had decided to kick her in the ass and I forgot all about my personal problems. I checked the status board and saw yellow lights flashing all along the aft end of the ship, including the main drives, the reactor and the hyperdrive. All a nice, cheerful, canary yellow and with a wonderful buzzing musical accompaniment to let me know they were serious. I threw the ship into a barrel roll, spinning her like a top to make it harder for the other guys to hit us in the same place twice. We were far enough up in Hanuman's gravity well that our ship's gravity field had taken over and I didn't feel the centripetal force, which was just as well, because just the sight of the view on the screen spinning around was making me motion-sick.

"Shoot at them, Delia," I told her, the words coming out strained as I began to imagine money flying out of my banking account on little wings. "Please shoot at them, as a favor to me?"

"It would be easier if the ship weren't rolling," she told me, but I saw her thumb push down on the trigger. She whooped in triumph and a look at the sensor display told me why.

The mercenary ship was breaking off, pulling away from us at top speed, a glowing red and white thermal bloom showing at the juncture of her port wing and fuselage, the tell-tale signs of an atmosphere leak. Beckett had nailed them good. Hope surged in my chest as I glanced from the threat display to the navigation board. We were at safe jump distance and there was no way they could latch back on before we were in hyperspace.

We'd made it, we were safe.

"Great job, Delia," I enthused. "Get ready to jump."

I had already fed in the coordinates for the Panicle, for Government Central. I jammed down the control to send us into hyperspace. Just a short, cross-system jump and we'd be home free. What could go wrong?

Well, about that…

Reality twisted into a Mobius strip and I had this vague sensation of being kicked in the groin by the universe over and over like I owed it money. I was strapped in, and I was fairly confident the artificial gravity hadn't failed, but I simultaneously felt as if I were drifting in the blackness of space...and then everything snapped back like a well-worn rubber band.

I tried to make my eyes focus. They didn't seem to want to work in conjunction with each other and everything was a blur and I could hear Beckett retching not too far away from me. I hope she'd used the spacesick bags. Behind the puking sounds, there was an insistent beeping, a warning tone from the ship's computer telling me I'd been a bad boy and the ship didn't like me anymore.

My vision swam back into clarity and I found out just how badly the ship disliked me. We were at the Panicle all right, only a few kilometers out from the massive collage of scrap metal. We were nowhere near the Government Center though. The mess below us was very familiar, unmistakable. It was El Mercado. That wouldn't have been a problem, normally. I could have contacted traffic control and requested a course to the Government Center, then fired up the drives and coasted on over there, just a few thousand kilometers away.

But...

"What's wrong?" Beckett asked. "What happened?"

"Slight misjump," I told her. "Nothing fatal. Just a couple little malfunctions."

"What's malfunctioning?" she demanded, wiping something yellow and disgusting off her chin.

"Communications," I said with a shrug. "Hyperdrive. Main engines. Reactor."

Her eyes widened with each word and I let her be scared because one of us should be able to let the fear show, and I couldn't afford to. Not yet. Something flashed on the screen, something about 20,000 kilometers away but I knew it immediately.

"Oh," I added, "and the bad guys? They just got here." I shrugged. "We may have a problem."

[12]

"Can't we call for help?"

Beckett had, for some reason, taken off her harness and was hanging over my right shoulder, staring at the command display as if the picture were any prettier from this side of the cockpit.

"We could," I said, trying to keep a tight rein on my temper because I so dearly wanted to curse right then. "Except for that whole part about our communications array being burned out."

"What are we going to do, then?"

"Mercado station," I called over the ship's commo board, ignoring Beckett. "Mercado station, this is the independent transport *Charietto* declaring an emergency. I have multiple system failures and I need to dock immediately."

I didn't wait for an answer, using the only propulsion I had available, the maneuvering thrusters, to kick the ship forward into a docking approach vector. It was just as well I didn't wait, because none was forthcoming.

"Why aren't they answering?" Beckett wondered.

"Gosh, I dunno," I said, trying to concentrate on following the suggested course projection on the navigation screen. It wasn't easy. I was a middling pilot and this was a job for an expert. "Maybe because El Mercado is run by criminals and their traffic control personnel are just as crooked as everyone else there, on sale to the highest bidder. And maybe they…" I pointed at the sensor display where the mercenary ship still shadowed us, not rushing in but not running away either. "…are bidding right now."

"Can't we make a counter-offer?" She was getting a bit shrill, close to panic, and I sympathized. I was on the ragged edge of panic myself.

"I got nothing but this ship and a robot Dog, lady," I said with a tightness across my chest that I told myself was from the damage to the ship. "And both are pretty much going to cost more to fix than they're worth at this point."

The only reason I wasn't more worked up about how much it would cost to repair the damage to my ship was the fact I was pretty sure I'd be dead long before the bill came due. That, and I was trying to dock with no guidance and no beacon.

"Mercado control, unless you tell me not to, I'm going to dock at the closest unoccupied bay. Please respond."

Nothing. My eyes flickered over to the reaction mass readout for the maneuvering thrusters and saw I had maybe another thirty seconds' worth of fuel. Grey walls were rising on either side of the *Charietto*, but I barely noticed them from the corner of my vision. My concentration was locked on the computer-simulated grid framework, its glowing lines trying to guide me into the empty docking bay between a cargo shuttle and a small courier.

This was the hard part. I had very little fuel left, which meant I had exactly one try to get the lock lined up with the umbilical, and I had to do it with one burn. Did I mention I was a middling pilot?

Metal scraped on metal and the vibration rattled the hull and set my teeth on edge, but then there was a solid thump and the light on the docking indicator flashed green. What was a few more scrapes when half the ship's systems were down? I blew out a breath and yanked loose my quick-release, scrambling out of the pilot's seat.

"Hurry!" I urged Beckett, pushing her ahead of me out of the cockpit. "We need to go!"

"Go where?"

I checked my gun belt. I'd had the gun at my hip when I'd sat down, but I was paranoid the blaster had slipped from its holster while I'd been in the acceleration couch. It was still there and I patted it for reassurance. I went to the utility cabinet and grabbed another blaster, handing it to Beckett.

"Keep that in your holster until I tell you it's time to pull it," I instructed her firmly. "I know you don't have much shooting experience and I'd rather not have you put a round into me or some innocent bystander, so you're going to keep your hands off this unless I say so. Right?"

She nodded, the motion a bit jerky, as if her neck was too tense to move naturally.

"But where are we going?" she repeated.

I ignored her again and went to where Dog lay motionless on the deck just past the belly ramp. We had very little time, but I just couldn't bring myself to leave him there like a discarded trash bag. I scooped him up in my arms carefully, as if he could feel the discomfort, his body feeling natural and lifelike except where his leg had been blown nearly off. It was jagged and metallic and it jabbed painfully into my bicep. I endured it and set him down gently on a fold-down acceleration couch, pausing, waiting for any sign of...well, not life, I suppose. Any sign he was aware of what was going on.

"Come on, you miserable cuss," I urged him. "Tell me how useless and stupid I am."

His eyes moved and I gasped. A stray spark flared from his mangled leg joint as he tried to move it, then stopped.

"Fuck, what did you let those assholes do to me, you useless meatsack?"

His voice was muted, distorted, as if he were speaking through a wall of cotton, and his mouth didn't move to match the words, but the question squeezed the breath out of me, somehow and I sagged against the chair.

"The ship's badly damaged," I told him, "and we're stuck on El Mercado with no comms. I have to take Beckett and try to get somewhere we can call for help. Do you want me to try to rig up a backpack to take you with us? Or can you walk on three legs?"

"I could walk on two legs, dumbass. But my power couplings are fried. I had to reroute three of the feeds just to get my voice synthesizer working again. I ain't going anywhere and I sure as hell ain't going to play Yoda sitting on your back while you run around doing backflips and swinging from vines."

"Play who?" I asked, frowning.

"Oh, good God, Masterson." There was disgust in his voice, even if it didn't reach his eyes due to the facial muscle fibers lacking power. "You really have to get a classical education. Get going before they catch your stupid ass sitting here like an idiot."

I nodded, realizing he was right but not liking it.

"Are you going to be okay here?" I felt stupid asking it, felt sure he was going to try to make me feel even *more* stupid.

"I'll be fine," he insisted, surprising me with his lack of insults. "I just need time for my internal repair systems to do their job. Cover me up with a blanket or something before you go."

I blinked, uncomprehending. "Are you...cold?"

"Don't be any more of a dumbass than genetics require, Masterson. If anyone manages to break into the ship while you're gone, I want them to think I'm an old suitcase or something, so they don't steal me and sell me off for spare parts."

"Right." I grabbed an old duffle bag out of the tiny closet under my bunk in my cabin, stripped a blanket off the bed and returned to lay them both gently atop Dog. "We'll be back as soon as we can," I assured him. It felt wrong leaving him there, felt like I was abandoning him, but we couldn't stay any longer.

"Yeah, yeah," he mumbled, his voice even more distant and muffled through the cover. I was pushing Beckett toward the airlock and barely caught his final words, spoken just as I hit the control to open the inner airlock and we stepped inside.

"Hey Grant…don't get killed."

It was the nicest thing he'd ever said to me.

———

There was something different about El Mercado. It was hard to put a finger on it, but I could sense it. The crowds were still there, as they were no matter what time of day it was. They had a nominal day-night cycle, a dimming of the exterior lights that didn't accomplish much except to give criminals a more psychologically welcoming environment to do bad things. It was night, but there were just as many beggars, pickpockets, street vendors and travelers as any other time I'd passed through the spaceport.

There was a tension in this night, though, something I could feel, could sense even if I couldn't have told you what gave me the impression. I thought for a moment it was just my own tension filtering my sensory input, making me paranoid, but I knew that wasn't it. Contrary to popular opinion, Marshals and others whose professions involve violence and the threat of violence don't have better instincts than anyone else. They're just more trained to listen to them.

I took a class on it in the Academy. We notice things subconsciously that never penetrate through to our thinking minds, subtle cues ingrained in us by millions of years hunting and being hunted on the African savannahs. Eyes meeting ours even if we couldn't quite make them out, heads turning in the periphery of our vision, sudden changes of movement meant to not be seen. They all merge together into a nagging feeling that something is not quite right.

And something was not quite right.

"They're watching us," I told Beckett, leaning back over my shoulder to make sure she heard me.

I'd told her to hang on to the rear of my gunbelt so we didn't get separated...and so she could watch our backs. It wasn't the most comfortable thing in the world, someone's fingers clenched around your belt, yanking you off balance at inopportune times, but I figured it was better than me turning around and finding out we'd been separated in the pressing crowd.

There was something else bothering me about the crowd. The usual beggars and drug dealers and vendors hawking their wares were all there, but not a one had tried to sell me anything or ask me for money. They actually moved out of our way as we pushed through the spaceport and not once did I have to block a hand from trying to snake into one of my pockets.

They knew who I was and they wanted no part of me tonight. It was like walking through a nightmare, but when we left the port and moved into the transportation hub, I felt no relief. The crowds in the port had been a sort of insulation around us, but once we were past the train station, it was stripped away and it seemed as if we were naked, bugs on a plate for the whole world to see.

"Where are we going?" Beckett asked, voice faint as she faced away from me, casting a longing look back at the trains.

I'd considered chancing the trains, hoping the armor of all the tourists and business travelers might keep us safe a little longer, but the possibility of being cornered in an enclosed train car and having a gunfight in the midst of all those...well, not *innocent* bystanders, but bystanders nonetheless...didn't appeal to me. I'd seen the results of indiscriminate gunfire in public and I didn't need anything else burdening my already strained conscience.

So, we walked. When I had passed through the tunnels and corridors and open streets of El Mercado before, I'd always thought of myself as an outsider, watching the degenerate squalor from above. I'd been a hunter, stalking my prey, unworried, untouchable. Now I was the hunted.

"There's a public communications hub near the center of this place," I told Beckett, finally answering her question. "It's not used much. The cartels and the gangs and the crime syndicates have their own secure ways of passing messages, the companies that actually do legal—or quasi-legal—business here have dedicated antennae they rent, and most everyone else wouldn't care enough about anything outside this station to bother making a call. But it's Union regulations that every space station have a public communications center, so it's there. We have to get to it and send a call out to Government Central, get the Marshals out here to pick us up."

I was talking to Beckett, but my eyes were on the passers-by. They were the usual clusters of young men and women—segregated by sex for mutual protection. There were boy gangs and there were girl gangs, but there were no mixed gangs. Any girls who hung out with the boy gangs were arm candy and vice versa. It was a fascinating sociological study and I'd read about universities sending in researchers to try to document it. Most of them had gotten themselves killed.

They were staring at us. Every eye on every young punk who passed turned our way, some careful to wait until they thought we wouldn't notice, some unabashed and unafraid. But they knew who we were, I was dead certain sure of it. I tried to walk faster, but all that wound up doing was getting me into trouble quicker.

The path to the Communications Center led through a utility tunnel, a joint between two sections of the station patched together roughly when it was originally being assembled from spare parts. It was a natural choke point, and the gangs knew it. One of them was waiting for us there. Boys. Seven of them, which would make them one of the smaller groups around here, or maybe this was all they could get together on short notice.

I slowed, then stopped, scanning the half-circle of them blocking our way. Their clothes were bright and flashy and hung off of them in a style that had become fashionable because it was supposed to be a call-back to when the underclass starved and their hand-me-down clothes hung off of them. Now, of course, there was free soy paste and spirulina powder and free autochefs to make it taste halfway decent, and free fabricator time and a lot of free clothing patterns and if anyone went hungry or wore hand-me-downs it was a style choice.

But anything to make yourself look like a victim, I suppose, particularly when you spend most of your time as a predator. I saw two guns among them, both black-market shotguns, but there might have been more concealed under untucked shirts or jackets. A few more had blades, their metal matte black and almost invisible in the dim light of the junction tunnel. Their eyes were cloaked in the shadows, as if they were trying to hide the fact they were human, maybe from us or maybe from themselves.

"We need to back up," I told Beckett, putting a hand on her arm and gently pushing her backward.

"Should I draw my gun now?" she hissed in my ear, slowly taking two steps back.

"No. Wait until we don't have any other choice."

Four more of them stepped out of the shadows at the other end of the tunnel, behind us, and I dragged Beckett to a sudden halt. I drew my blaster, keeping it at my side.

"Nobody has to get hurt here," I said, loudly and clearly, eyes darting back and forth between the two groups. "Just get out of the way and let us through."

"'Fraid we can't do that, vato," one of them said, shaking his head in mock sadness. He was the tallest of them, maybe three or four centimeters taller than me, though probably the same weight. He had a shotgun tucked under his arm as if it were a fashion accessory. "You ain't going nowhere."

"What's your name, kid?" I asked him, keeping my voice steady.

"My name's Fuck You," he replied with a sneer.

"Okay, Mr. You," I returned, "I know there's just the two of us and you fellas have eleven, but let me tell you how this is going to go down. The second anyone makes a move toward us, I kill you." I raised the blaster slowly and settled the barrel in a line for the kid's chest. "No questions asked, don't matter who actually moved, you get it first, because you're the leader and you got a gun."

"It don't matter if I...," he started to spout some sort of bravado, but I cut him off.

"*Then* I'm going to kill anyone else holding a weapon," I continued. "And if you think you can get to me before I do, well..." I nudged Beckett. She stared at me without comprehension and I sighed. "Draw your gun now, Delia," I told her quietly.

She nodded and fumbled the blaster out of its holster, holding it at an awkward high ready.

"She ain't as good a shot as I am," I confessed, "but she don't have to be. She'll just watch my back and spray pure hellfire at anyone who gets too close." I grinned. "At this range, she can't miss."

I was seriously hoping the bluff would work...mostly because it wasn't a bluff. It was exactly what we'd have to do if they attacked, except I was going to try not to kill the ones I had to shoot. That was a chancy thing when you're putting a blast of plasma into a human body, though. Even a hit to the leg or shoulder can do enough damage for someone to die of shock before they get to a medic.

The one who'd spoken seemed to be considering it seriously, licking his lips with the nervous energy of a lizard in the sun. I thought he was sweating, but it was too dark to be sure.

He made the wrong decision.

"Get 'em!" he yelled, obviously thinking this was going to be like a movie, or maybe like one of the other strong-arm jobs his gang had done before. He raised the shotgun one-handed, like an idiot.

I blew his right hand off. He screamed, falling backwards onto his butt, cradling the blackened, charred stump to his chest, the shotgun clattering to the ground. Everyone else stared, as if the horrible wound was a slap to the face, waking them up from the dream-like idea they could take me. Well, not everyone. The other guy with a gun, probably a close buddy of Mr. Fuck You, got off a shot. The flechettes, or birdshot, or whatever it was ricocheted off the pavement and hit nothing I could tell because he was panicked.

He was even more panicked when I shot him in the left foot. More screaming, more rolling on the ground in pain. I shot twice more in quick succession and blasted the shotguns to melted slag before anyone else could think to try to pick them up. Then I holstered my gun and smiled broadly to hide the churning in my stomach.

I'd maimed two teenagers. They could recover, if they sought immediate treatment. The hand and the foot could be grown back. And it was the least violent solution to the problem that I could think of on short notice, but none of that made me feel any better about it. And now I had to try to bluff my way through the rest so I wouldn't have to shoot anyone else.

"I'm feeling generous today," I told them, keeping my face and voice hard and implacable. "I didn't kill anyone...yet. Get your friends to the clinic before they die of shock and maybe we can keep it that way."

Feet shuffled and a chorus of muted mumbling accompanied their slow and ignominious retreat, punctuated by the screams of the two wounded kids as they were hoisted up between their friends. In seconds, they were all out of sight. Except for one.

He was the youngest of the group, his hair a mass of tangled, mismatched styles and colors, his expression fearless and petulant.

"It won't matter," he declared, brash and unafraid. He jabbed a finger in our general direction. "You're both still dead."

"How would you know, kid?" I asked, unimpressed. It was easy to risk your life when you'd hardly even lived. That was why wars were fought by the young.

He pulled something out of his jacket pocket and I tensed, thinking it was a weapon. It was a folding tablet, one of the cheap, recyclable ones they give away at public entertainment centers. He tapped the screen to bring it back to life and turned it around so I could see.

It was us. Beckett and me. Our pictures, mine from my bounty hunter license, Beckett's from her wanted file. I didn't know the page he'd pulled up, but it was undoubtedly part of the local underground network, the encrypted and anonymous tangle of nooks and crannies hidden in the free public nets where criminals could advertise and brag and exchange services. Beside our photos and files, there was a price.

I whistled soft and low.

"Is that a comma or a decimal point?" Beckett asked, her eyes wide, her face pale.

It was a study in irony. I had a bounty on my head.

The boy laughed, the sound high-pitched and manic. His eyes were feverish and I knew he had to be on something. But then, they all were.

"Enjoy the rest of your life, assholes."

And then he was gone, melting back into the shadows with the rest of them, and we were alone.

"We're dead," Delia Beckett said so softly I barely heard her even in the still silence.

"That," I admitted, "is a distinct possibility."

[13]

CONGRESS with the Beast hadn't changed at all in the few weeks since I'd last enjoyed its hospitality, but my reception at the front door was less warm and welcoming than last time.

"Give me one fucking reason," Nikki Cortez snarled behind the muzzle of the shotgun, "why I shouldn't just kill you right now, lawman."

My eyes flickered from one side of the entrance hall to the other, noting the position and weaponry of each of the three bouncers Nikki had called in the minute she'd seen me. They weren't the same ones I'd seen last time, which probably meant she'd had to hire new ones after our little dust-up. Two women and a man this time, all around the same height, all three with shaven heads and matching black suits in what seemed like an effort to make them look more professional. The women carried sawed-off shotguns similar to the one Nikki was holding on us, while the man had a compact handgun, a slug-shooter from the looks of it.

I still felt confident in my ability to take out all three of them if it came down to it, but that wasn't why I was here. I noticed

Beckett's hand flirting with the blaster at her hip and I shot her a warning look.

"I'm not a lawman, Ms. Cortez," I reminded her. "I'm just a bounty hunter. I didn't get your ex-husband in trouble, I just did what I got paid to do. And if you talk to Abel, he'll tell you I treated him fair and tried to give him as good advice as I could."

"I don't give a shit if you tucked him in at night and read him a Goddamned bedtime story, cowboy!" Nikki snapped, bringing the shotgun barrel even closer to my face. "What do you want with me?"

"I need your help," I told her, bracing myself for the flood of scornful laughter I knew would soon follow.

She didn't disappoint.

"And why would I want to help you?" she asked once she'd gotten her breath back from the hysterical cackling. She was not a pleasant person, but she'd gone out of her way to try to help her ex-husband, which showed she must have a special place in her heart for fools and the weak-minded. "There's a reward for your heads that could pay off my mortgage on this hole and let me finally sell it off to some sucker and move out of El Mercado. Why shouldn't I take it?"

"You'd get the money," I allowed, "and you'd also get the blood it's coated with." I cocked an eyebrow at her. "You've been around the block. You know nothing comes that free or easy. People are gonna hear about this. The Marshals already know what bounty I'm here to bring in and they know I was heading for Government Central. You don't think the Marshals have an AI running through the nets round the clock?"

I shook my head. "They may not find out who's behind this with both of us dead, but they'll damn sure know who ratted us out. How long you think you'll have to enjoy the reward before they lock you up for conspiracy to commit murder?"

That seemed to hit her where she lived, and I could see the barrel of the shotgun waver just slightly.

"Let's say you're right about that," she said, just the slightest crack in her mask of belligerence. "That still don't mean I should help you. I could just kick both your asses back out into the street and be done with you."

"You say you want money, right?" I prodded. "Clean money you can do something with?" I held my hands up, palms out. "I got a bounty coming from Ms. Beckett here, a sizable one. It's yours if you hide us out for a few hours and help me get a message to the Marshals at Government Central."

Nikki frowned, the gun slipping even farther downward.

"How sizable?"

I pulled out a folding tablet from my jacket and scrolled through its menu until I found where I had downloaded the open bounty, then passed it over to her. Her eyebrow went up at the amount.

"And you'd sign *all* that over to me?"

"The minute you put the call in to Government Central," I promised. "As soon as I hear the Marshals are on their way to pick us up, the money's yours."

Nikki was silent for a long moment, then she caught the bouncers' attention and jerked her head back toward the front door. The three of them seemed to relax slightly before moving out back to the entrance.

"All right, cowboy, you've got a deal. But on one condition." At my questioning look, she continued. "If those fucking animals out there figure out where you went, if they come in here after you, the deal's off. I'll hide you out here for a little bit, but I ain't shedding any blood for you."

"Fair enough," I agreed. "Where do you want us?"

———

"This is fucking creepy," Delia Beckett said, pulling her knees up to her chest, trying to get farther away from the deactivated pleasure dolls crowding around us.

We were back in the repair and storage room where I'd found and arrested Abel Schiff not all that long ago, and yes, the irony was not lost on me. The lights were dim and we were both squatting in a dark corner, the robots sprawled out on the floor on either side of us, their legs stretched out like we were all taking part in some disaster drill. Some were naked, some clothed provocatively, others stripped of their flesh, horrifying metal skeletons staring at us in the dark.

"Yeah, it's not my favorite place," I admitted, "but at least it's a shot at getting out of this without anyone else shooting at us."

"Do you think you can really count on this Nikki to help us? You arrested her husband."

"Ex-husband," I corrected her absent-mindedly, my eyes exploring the room from my seat by the wall. "And no, I don't guess I'm really counting on her to make the call, though it'd be nice. But staying out on the street would have been suicide." I finally hit on what I was looking for, a portable programming stand for the robots, nestled into a corner on four round casters. "Delia, can I ask you a personal question?"

She blinked, shook her head at the sudden shift of conversational gears.

"Sure, I guess."

"Have you ever programmed a pleasure doll?"

———

Not only could Delia Beckett program a doll, she also had the computer know-how to tap into the brothel's security monitors using the neglected data terminal half-hanging off the wall, its left-hand mount broken. I didn't remember it being that way when

I'd arrested Schiff. Maybe the tech they'd hired to replace him had anger issues.

"Where'd you learn this hacking stuff?" I wondered. "I thought you worked in the shipping department."

"Jake taught me," she said, tracing a command line on the touch screen as she held it upright with her other hand. A shadow passed across her face at the mention of her ex-lover's name and I wondered if she'd ever get over him. Then again, I still hadn't gotten over Janie, so who was I to talk? "He used to hack into the entertainment net at Hadur and reprogram the filters so we could watch this ridiculous computer animation show he loved. It was supposed to be written by an illegal Artificial Intelligence, so it was proscribed by the company, but it was probably just a couple of college kids making up the silliest, most awkward shit they could think of."

"Yeah," I said, nodding as a memory nagged at the back of my mind. "That's...Panomi, right? My son used to watch that."

"You have a son?" she asked him. "Are you married?"

The air went out of me in a soft hiss. "I was. My wife left me right about the same time as I lost my job as a Marshal, and took Luke with her. I haven't seen him in..." I squeezed my eyes shut, not wanting to share the tears welling up there with anyone else. "...a good long time now."

"Why did you lose your job?" she asked, voice subdued and solicitous yet also curious. Maybe she wanted to know what sort of man she was trusting with her life. "You seem pretty good at this sort of thing."

"There was a senior Union Representative named Tomas Caty," I told her, realizing we hadn't gotten around to that story yet, "who kept coming up on my radar in chatter from arms dealers we were monitoring. I looked into it and it seemed as if a lot of hijacked arms shipments we investigated had passed through his office at one time or another. So, I decided to look into him, but I was expressly told to back off."

"But you didn't," she guessed, turning the terminal screen around in her hands and pulling off a panel to expose circuitry. "You have a multitool handy?"

I nodded, fishing the instrument out of a pouch on my gun belt and handing it to her.

"No, I didn't," I confirmed. "I was keeping it quiet, thought I was being clever. Trying to work it into my normal investigations by concentrating on the suspected illegal weapons smugglers who I had a hunch were involved with Caty. My partner knew what I was doing and tried to warn me, but I couldn't let it go. And when Caty's name finally came up in an exchange between the smuggler and his source, I skipped my commander and went straight to Caty's office and tried to question him about it." I chuckled softly, trying to keep the bitterness from welling up again. "That went about as well as you might expect. And after his lawyers kicked me out on my ass, I got called into my captain's office and threatened with demotion and reassignment if I didn't back off."

"And you still didn't?" Her eyes went wide.

"I didn't have the chance. Caty's data protection techs claimed they found monitoring software on his systems and that I was the only one who could have installed it. They tried to press charges, tried to get me fired." I pressed my thumb and forefinger to either side of my head, rubbing at a sudden pain in my temples. "I told everyone I didn't do it, but he'd managed to penetrate the central systems and leave a trail of data bread crumbs all pointed back at me. I was going to get demoted, reassigned, it would kill any chance of promotion for years to come. And I messed up. I went to his office and punched him in the face. And that was it, my career was over, my marriage was over. And I couldn't even contest the custody of my son because I'd had to plead guilty to misdemeanor assault to avoid jail time."

"Sorry."

I grinned. I couldn't help it. She was looking at life in prison for treason, if the various people trying to kill us didn't succeed first, and she was sorry my life had gone off the rails. She seemed to get the joke, too, because she laughed, almost unwillingly, before her attention went back to her work.

"Got it," she announced, closing the panel on the back of the display and turning it back around to scroll through a menu. "And here's the feed from the security system…"

She trailed off and one look at the screen told me why. The first of the multiple sub-displays was the front entrance, where we'd been intercepted by the bouncers. There were five strangers standing in the entrance hall, four men and a woman, and they weren't locals. You could tell by their clothes, by their hairstyles. They screamed corporate in their dark-colored, thousand-credit business suits that weren't exactly uniforms but close enough. They were tailored well enough you couldn't even see their guns until they pulled them out and pointed them in Nikki's face.

"Those aren't the guys from the street," Beckett said. I tried not to roll my eyes at the statement of the obvious.

"Those," I informed her, my gut roiling, "are the guys from that ship that followed us here. Those are corporate mercenaries, if I'm not mistaken. Former military, probably from the 82 Eridani system. The peace deal put them out of work, but not for long."

Nikki had her hands up, the usual pugnacious defiance gone from her eyes in the face of the professional killers.

"If she's good to her word," Beckett said, "we're fucked."

"Get everything ready," I said, looking around the room, trying to find the best place to hide.

I'd been doing that since we arrived here without much luck and the situation hadn't improved. There was a storage closet, but it was stacked with crates of spare parts that would have taken a half hour to move and left a way-too-obvious pile of boxes sitting in the middle of the floor.

"It's all set up," she told me, tapping a final control on the screen before she pressed the button on the side to turn off the display. "As long as your 'link is putting out the signal, we'll be fine."

Somehow, plunging into the task of hacking into the brothel's systems had distracted her from the fear and anxiety and somewhere along the line, she'd become calmer than me. Which was embarrassing, given that I was supposed to be the hardened, callous bounty hunter.

"Over here," I decided, motioning for her to join me in the far corner of the room.

I drew my blaster and crouched down, trying to blend in with a row of pleasure dolls locked upright and leaning against the faded, cracked wall. Beckett squeezed beside me, warm and human in contrast to the lifelessness of the robots, robbed of even the illusion of reality.

"Do you think you can get them all?" she wondered, staring at the dull metal emitter of the gun.

"I doubt I'll get any," I confessed. "If things go the way we hope, there's going to be too much stuff between us and them. But I don't want to die for lack of shooting back."

"Should I take out my gun?"

"No. They might bring Nikki in here with them and I don't want to risk shooting her by accident."

I knew they were coming, which was probably why it seemed to take forever for them to get here. I concentrated on controlling my breathing, not wanting the movement of my shoulders to give away our position the second they walked in. Would they just walk in shooting wildly, blasting the whole room? Did they want Beckett alive?

"They were in here a few minutes ago." That was Nikki, her

voice coming from just outside the door, a bit too loudly for it to be a mistake. She was trying to warn us, for which I gave her some ethical credit.

At least I wouldn't have to hand my bounty over to her...

The door burst open and one of the mercenaries rolled through on her shoulder, compact blaster held out in front of her. I made not a sound nor a move, trusting the shadows and the sex bots to keep me hidden. The woman was slim and short and looked like she weighed no more than forty-five kilos, but there was a razor-sharp edge to her face and what I'd come to think of in my career as killer's eyes, cold and dark and dead. She'd put a round through my head and not lose a wink of sleep about it, if I let her.

Behind her, the others filed through the door, peeling off one at a time to different sides of the room. When the last one came through, it was movement enough to trigger the dolls. That had been the tricky part, the part Beckett had labored at for nearly an hour, how to get the dolls to activate when we needed them to without us having to move, to push a button or speak a command or anything else that would draw attention—and gunfire—in our direction.

I'd thought of motion detection, knowing the dolls must have the sensors for it. Beckett had wondered how I'd known so much about pleasure dolls, but some things you just pick up when you do this job.

The doll we'd chosen was unassuming, rather restrained given the nature of the place. No leather, no frilly lingerie, no physiologically unlikely anatomy. Just a fairly normal-looking simulacrum of a younger woman with bobbed red hair, wearing an oversized T-shirt, just in case anyone got sentimental about their first college girlfriend, I supposed. She looked up, smiling an eerie, lifelike smile and launched herself off the repair table without a sound.

To their credit, none of the hit team screamed like three-year-olds. *I* would have screamed like a three-year-old. The closest to the table was a broad-shouldered, smooth-faced man with slicked-back brown hair and pinched features, eyes too close together, mouth too high. He'd been designed by nature rather than a genetics lab, his parents probably working stiffs on Dagda. He threw himself backwards, teeth clenched, and fired his blaster instinctively, one-handed.

It was a hell of a shot, especially under stress, and it sheered the top of the redhead's skull clean off in a shower of sparks. Unfortunately for pinch-face, pleasure dolls don't keep their power supplies or CPUs in their head. Just because humans are forced by evolution to put everything vital in such an exposed spot doesn't mean robot designers are.

Where a mop of red hair had been was now a shower of sparks and a halo of white smoke and the robot was *howling*, and I wondered why it would be programmed to howl but then decided I didn't want to know. It slammed into pinch-face and wrapped his torso into a loving, inescapable embrace and he squawked as the air went out of his chest. The others were moving to help, but they'd been so wrapped up in stopping the redhead that they hadn't noticed the rest of the sex bots.

Some, of course, had been too damaged or disassembled to get them functioning, but every pleasure doll with a charge in their power pack and a working CPU moved, surging forward as one…and so did we. Metal and fake flesh and high heels clapped against the tile floor and two dozen generic come-ons blended into a wordless gabble, an undertone to the shouts and the crashing of work tables and an endless flash-crack of blaster fire.

The shots were un-aimed, wild, panicked, and any one of them could have hit Beckett and me. I slitted my eyes against the flare of plasma energy and followed the press of the pleasure dolls, Beckett's hand in mine, my blaster at the ready in case I had a shot. All I saw was the bare flesh on the back of the sex bots and I wasn't ready to fire at random hoping to hit something because not attracting attention was sort of the whole point.

I shouldered aside thrashing bodies and couldn't tell if they were human or robot, could barely tell when we burst through the doorway into the hall outside because everything was spilling out of the room with us. There were shouts and exclamations and doors were swinging open up and down the hallway, heads popping out like prairie dogs, and people started to run.

Bodies crowded around and I pulled Beckett closer to me, lowering my shoulder and pushing like I was back on the high school football team, trying to get a first down on third and inches. People or robots or whatever was in front of me moved, not just from the pressure of my shoulder but also from the urge to get out of the building. The entrance hallway was meters away and I could see the glare of advertising placards out in the street, and I thought we were home free.

Then pinch-face was right in front of me, a bruise already forming on the right side of his cheek from something, anger in his beady eyes and a blaster pointed our way.

I shot from instinct, from training, but that training betrayed me. I aimed center mass, harder to miss at the middle of his chest, but these were professionals and he was wearing body armor underneath that fancy suit. The jacket and vest and shirt burned away with a fringe of flame and a puff of smoke, but the slate grey of the energy armor was still visible beneath it and the man didn't go down, just staggered backwards from the heat.

And then we were out, pouring into the street in a wash of humanity and running alongside the crowd. Guilt twisted my stomach, guilt at using innocent civilians for cover, but abandoning the throng meant heading right back into the teeth of the hit team, and I couldn't bring myself to do that to Beckett.

I risked a look back and saw the business suits filtering through the crowd, a few dozen meters back but still coming, inexorable, inescapable. A blaster fired from somewhere behind me and the energy beam splashed against a wall with an explosion of liberated water vapor and an antiphonal chorus of screams. People ducked, scattered, ran even faster, and so did we. My pulse pounded in my ears, my breath chuffing and uncontrollable, and I was caught up in the panic of the masses, but running through the crowd was a temporary solution, guaranteed to get us and others wounded or killed.

I spotted the signs for the local train station and made a split-second decision, mostly because the crowd was heading the opposite direction. The entrance was an archway over a tunnel seven meters wide and three high, the active display advertising proudly that this was Station 540A and it served the southwest section of El Mercado.

"We're getting on the train?" Beckett asked breathlessly, sticking close by my left shoulder, having to run to match my jog down the steps to the station.

"No," I said, but didn't elaborate. "Just stay with me and keep low."

The clamor and motion of the street faded behind us as the entrance to the underground station swallowed us up.

THE TERMINAL WAS A CAVE, not wreathed in shadows but in neon light, casting everything in an artificial aura of cartoonish color. The station had two platforms, twin tracks, and there weren't more than a dozen people queued up for either of them, but neither train was in the station at the moment. Which was perfect. I didn't know this particular station, but I was very familiar with ones like it throughout the Union, on back-woods colonies and cut-rate space stations just like this one, places where high tech and high maintenance were too expensive.

No evacuated tunnels, no magnetic suspension, just rails and wheels…and space for us to run and hide. I blew past a cluster of older, beat-down looking locals, their clothes drab and simple, their expressions disinterested even when they saw us both jumping down off the platforms onto the track. I hit hard plastic lining on the balls of my feet and fell into a crouch, then nearly toppled over when Beckett plowed into me from the side.

The neon yellow of the station lights faded to a shadowy grey in the looming tunnel, the only illumination coming from chemical strip lights in circles along the tubular walls and alongside the tracks. I pushed away from the floor lining and came to my feet, grabbing Beckett and yanking her up with me.

"What…," she began, but the words ended in a muted shriek when a plasma blast splashed against the far wall of the tunnel.

There were no more questions nor the time to answer them. I pushed her ahead of me along the maintenance walkway, a narrow strip of metal grating beside the tracks, and wished she could run faster. I could have run faster, and I was fairly sure the bad guys chasing us had not skimped on the cardio either. I pulled my blaster and held it out behind me, glancing back over my shoulder every few steps.

One of those glances revealed a shape backlit by the yellow glow of the terminal and I fired at it without stopping to aim, more interested in keeping their heads down than stopping and getting into a standing gunfight. I fired off a burst of four shots, hoping to God I hit something, and then my charge went dry. I should have expected it, should have already switched out power packs, but I'd made a rookie mistake and lost track.

I briefly considered trying to reload on the run or, alternatively, having Beckett pass me her gun, but two things changed my mind. The first was a stinging, burning swarm of sparks from a blaster shot impacting the wall beside us, and the second was the light and wailing horn of an oncoming train.

"Shit!" Beckett said, and I couldn't have put it better myself.

This time she saved the day, because my eyes were full of afterimages from the blaster shot and I couldn't see a thing. I felt her pulling me to the side, to the wall and past it, and I realized we were in some sort of darkened alcove. I didn't know what it was for, and I wasn't about to try to speculate at the moment, but I used the time to reload. My eyes hadn't adjusted and there wasn't even a hint of light in the niche in the wall, so I ejected the spent power pack by feel and inserted a new one.

The old one went into the pouch where the fresh one had

come from. The things aren't cheap, and I wasn't back in the Marshals where we could toss them anywhere and let the government buy me a new one. The process reminded me of my tactical training in the Academy, where they shut off the lights and played distracting noises to force you to work under pressure.

Pressure was being provided in this case by a big, honking passenger train passing less than a meter in front of my face, the clacking of its wheels on the track a metallic heartbeat, the wind of its passage a hot breath in my face. I wanted to ask Beckett if she was all right, but I couldn't even hear myself think and I resolved to wait until the train had gone by before pressing on, sure there was no way the hit team could get to me with the sides of the cars only ten centimeters or so from the walls on each side.

I should have learned not to be that sure of anything. The only light I had was the flash of dim interior lamps through the windows of the train, just enough to reveal the blackness of a dark-clad silhouette and the glint of reflected light from the matte finish of a blaster. There wasn't time for coherent thought, just reaction, and my first reaction was my left hand striking out and seizing his right, trying to control the weapon before he could level it at us.

The man was strong and the pressure against my shoulder almost made me forget my own blaster. It was only a single moment's delay, but it was enough for him to secure my right wrist in the grip of his free hand and we were wrestling for control of the weapons and of each other in a space the size of a coffin with someone else jammed behind us and certain death less than a meter in front of us.

I should have yelled at Beckett to shoot him, but I was using all my breath and concentration against his not inconsiderable muscles, and that was on top of the fact I was severely worried she'd shoot me by accident. I didn't say a word. My chin was pressed into my chest and our foreheads were pressed against each other like a couple slow-dancing, each of us trying to protect from a headbutt by the other.

I was worried about Beckett, worried about the guns, too worried to take a risk. The corporate mercenary was less risk-averse. He stepped into a knee strike at my thigh and even though I turned and caught most of it on my hip, it was enough to knock me off balance and give him just the opening he needed.

I was turning, spinning, afraid to fire my gun for fear of hitting Beckett, being pushed back towards the train. The noise of the passing cars was deafening, each gap between them a gaping maw ready to swallow me up. It wasn't slowing and I had the sense it wasn't stopping at this terminal, was intent on proceeding straight through to the next, so there was no hope of respite.

The emitter of my blaster struck the side of the train and, as I tried to hold onto it anyway, my right wrist snapped. I would like to say that I bellowed with rage like a wounded bear, but the truth is, I screamed. There was anger in it, and pain, lots of pain, and fear, and desperation, and I used all of it, used the ten-kilo weight advantage I had on the guy and twisted him around with my hand on his wrist and my shoulder pressed into his.

I lunged into a front kick to his chest, my foot snapping like a piston. He flew backwards and, in this case, backwards was right into one of the gaps between the train cars. He was gone in the blink of an eye, a metallic crunch the only hint of his fate.

"Shit!" I yelled, clutching at my wrist, suddenly giving up on giving up swearing. "Goddammit, that hurts!"

And that was just as long as I could afford to indulge in the pain. The second the train was gone, the others would be coming for us, and I sucked at shooting with my left hand.

"Stay flat against the wall," I yelled in Beckett's ear, edging out into the tunnel, the train cars so close I could feel a loose strap from the collar of my jacket snapping against the metal.

I couldn't look back at the woman, couldn't turn my head at

all, couldn't even hold her hand because my wrist was throbbing like it had just got hit by a damned train, and I could only hope she'd developed enough instincts for self-preservation over the last couple years to blow out her breath and hug that wall. I don't know how many cars the train had but they seemed to go on forever, the rhythmic click-clack pounding in my head, the heartbeat of this decrepit cesspool of a space colony.

And then it was gone and I nearly collapsed forward, sucking in a long breath to try to steady myself. I grabbed at Beckett's arm with my left hand and pulled her ahead of me, pausing for just a moment to grab the gun from her holster.

"There," I said, pointing with the gun at a strip of red lighting along the wall, indicating an emergency exit. "Hurry."

I ran, and tried to think about anything other than the pain and swelling in my wrist and the interesting shade of purple it was already turning, and the way it felt as if someone was closing it in a vice with another turn for each step. I wasn't succeeding too well. The door was locked but it wasn't a fancy sort of lock with magnetic seals or biometrics. Nothing in this place was fancy or high-end. Everything was thrown together from leavings, kludged out of spare parts. I levelled the blaster, turned my head away, and fired a round through the bolt.

On the other side was a ladder and I cursed again, deciding to get as much mileage as I could from this lapse in my manners. I didn't want to take the time to pull my holster around to the opposite hip, so I just shoved the blaster into my jacket pocket and started climbing one-handed. I didn't know how much time we'd bought with the train, or how long the hit team would take confirming their friend's death.

Did they like him? Was he a fun guy to go out drinking with between murder missions? Would they stop to say something over the body of their friend? Or was it just business and they'd raise an eyebrow at his battered corpse and move on. I was hoping he was very popular and mourning would give us more time to get away, but that might have been shock setting in.

The ladder only stretched up ten meters but it could have been a million kilometers according to the itch between my shoulder blades. Getting shot in the ass would have been an undignified way to go, and the fact they'd have to go through Beckett to get to me didn't make me feel any better about it.

I guess the hit team must have liked pinched-face at least a little bit, because I hit the hatch without getting shot, though I almost did fall back down the ladder when I tried to open it one-handed. I wedged a foot against the opposite wall of the tunnel and grabbed at the latch, leaning into it to push it away from me. The door opened downward and almost knocked me off the ladder again, but I managed to grab onto one of the ladder rungs and pull myself up with one last surge of energy.

I was in an alley between two buildings stretching up all the way to the distant ceiling, fifty meters up, with barely a gap between their roofs and the light panels. I pulled Beckett up with my left hand, my right arm cradled against my chest, then I kicked the hatch shut and slammed my boot heel down on the latch handle, hoping I could jam it.

"Oh, thank God," she hissed, looking back down through the hatch as if she couldn't believe we were alive. "We made it."

I was looking elsewhere. The lights were still low, but people were out, crowds of them. Not families, not children. Just adults, mostly men, hanging off of balconies, standing in the street, drinking or openly smoking or injecting drugs.

They were watching.

"Don't be thanking anyone just yet," I told her. "We just went out of the frying pan and right back into the fire."

[15]

"WE HAVE to get out of sight," I told Beckett.

We'd only been walking for a few minutes since escaping the underground and things seemed to get worse with every step. My hands were a bit twitchy, I'll admit, and I was shaking from the constant, throbbing pain in my wrist. But Beckett was in full-blown post-adrenaline-rush jitters mode, her teeth clenched, eyes darting about like a ferret on amphetamines.

That wasn't the worst of it though. The worst part was, her paranoia was completely justified. The hit team was somewhere back behind us, and they'd be following soon if they weren't already. Everyone we saw on the street was staring at us, pulling out their 'links and making calls, and I was sure we'd picked up at least three different tails. I figured the only reason no one had taken another run at us was they didn't want to be the first to get shot, and now they *knew* I'd shoot them. At some point, I'd have to convince them I'd kill them, but I was hoping to put that off. I kept my left hand in my pocket, wrapped around the blaster's grip.

"Where could we go," Beckett asked me, her voice wavering,

a muscle in her cheek twitching, "on this tin can? There are people *everywhere.*"

I hadn't thought about that, but it made sense. She'd grown up on an isolated, sparsely-populated colony world. She wasn't just afraid of getting killed, she was getting phobic about the crowds.

What do they call that again? Not agoraphobia, that's fear of open spaces. If Dog were here, he'd know.

"I can only think of one place," I said. "The gravity generation array. It's three levels down, near the outer hull antipolar to the system primary. Everyone avoids it because of the radiation."

I didn't think it was possible, but her eyes got wider.

"Radiation? What radiation?"

"It's not fatal…I mean, I guess it would be if you lived right next to it for a few years, but you can go down there for short periods and not get anything worse than a headache."

"What about calling for help?" she reminded me. "I thought we had to call for help."

Before I could answer, I looked around to our right out of some sixth sense, some subconscious realization from the direction of the people around us, the echoes of the sound in the approaching intersection in the corridor. The streets were wide in this section, built like a planetside city to make tourists feel more at home, and the tourists I could pick out of the crowd were slowing, looking at something, while the locals were turning, making for the left-hand side of the road and shelter in the family bakery at the corner there.

I didn't want to look, didn't want to know. I just wanted to run. I looked anyway.

These were no kids, no teenage gangbangers. This was the real deal, the sort of muscle the people who ran El Mercado could call up on short notice. They were older, bigger, more professional, with none of the colorful, flashy clothing the kids had worn. Dark colors blended in with the shadows, and heavy jackets testified of the armor plating sewn into them. Haircuts were short and practical for men and women both, and there was no segregation by sex as in the youth gangs.

And there were a lot more guns. They didn't hold them out in the open, but I knew where to look and I could see the places they were being carried, the bulges beneath the clothes, the reassuring pats against the chest or side of heavy jackets. These guys wouldn't be intimidated and I wouldn't be able to shoot everyone holding a gun before they got me. Probably. I wasn't ready to try it, not unless our backs were against the wall.

I tried not to stare as I counted, but I couldn't help it. There were an even dozen of them, about two hundred meters away, and I could see them scanning the streets, looking for us.

I grabbed Beckett's hand and ran like Satan himself was on our heels.

She nearly stumbled at first, unprepared for the sudden acceleration, but I slowed down just enough for her to get her footing. I heard a distant yell behind us and didn't look back to see who it was, just headed the opposite direction from the street muscle. Pavement slapped against the soles of my boots and Beckett's heels scraped behind me, her palm sweating against mine and tugging me backwards with every step.

I wanted to look back and make sure she was okay, that she wasn't about to trip and yank us both down, but I was trying to piece together a street map of El Mercado in my head with one side of my brain, and with the other half, keep a watch out for any amateur bounty hunters ready to take us down and try to keep the reward for themselves.

The terrain here didn't help my navigation at all. Someone, long ago, had decided it would be a wonderful idea to build everything in this district in the style of a South American favela. Some historically-ignorant romanticist, I figured, because they'd gotten their idea of what a favela was from old movies instead of history books. They weren't, contrary to the popular culture of the last few decades, romantic and quaint neighborhoods with cozy little families sharing their dinner with local children and breaking into dance numbers in response to any personal drama.

They weren't tall and cramped and jammed together out of some stylistic aesthetic, they were symbols of neglect and corruption, abandoned by their governments and left to rot. They were poverty, and crime, and bodies being dumped every night and collapsing infrastructure, and they'd been that way right up till the time the Union was formed. Some were still that way.

I wasn't sure if it was history repeating itself or simply the same recipe being cooked with the same ingredients in two different ovens, but El Mercado's favelas were just as corrupt and abandoned and crime-ridden…and just as jumbled and confusing. Every one of them was slightly different, but not different enough to make an impression on me when I'd looked at a map.

All I knew was the service stairway down to the maintenance levels was in the alleyway between building A120 and A121, and if there were ever any numbers *anywhere* on these row houses, they certainly weren't there now. I suppose they could have been buried beneath the graffiti, or covered by hanging laundry, and I could have found them by letting my 'link scan the area and guide me with its mapping subroutines, but stopping to do that seemed like a great way to collect a bullet or energy blast in the back of the head.

Children crowded the railings of the last two or three levels of the row-houses, pointing at us and laughing, chattering in three or four different languages, only two of which I understood. The gist filtered downward through layers of noise and sweat and hard breathing and preoccupation: they were taking bets on how long before the two of us died.

I'll take some of that action. Give me five credits on 0300 local time.

I don't know how I saw the alley. It looked like any of a dozen others I'd passed in the last two minutes, and my attention to find detail was suffering with fatigue, but something caught my eye, just a shape somewhere down at the end of it, a light at the end of shadowed darkness.

It was the maintenance stairwell. I don't know how I knew, but I did, and I yanked Beckett after me, nearly pulling her off her feet. She stumbled and I skidded across something wet and tried not to think about what it might be, catching her shoulder before she fell into the unidentified puddle. The alley was dark but the service door was marked with a chemical strip light and I thought the subdued glow was probably what had drawn my eye to it.

Beckett looked a question at me, too out of breath to speak. I caught the meaning. Was this really a good idea?

"I don't know," I admitted. "It's the best idea I have."

I guess that was enough for her, or maybe she just didn't have the energy to think of something smarter, because she followed me down the thirty meters of narrow alleyway as if the strip of light over the metal door was the entryway to paradise.

Something jumped between a pair of plastic trash bins off to our left and my blaster fairly leapt out of my pocket, my trigger finger already beginning to press down before I saw it was a cat. Real, live dogs, they didn't have many of on space stations, but there were cats galore, because wherever we went, however careful we were about it, humans always seemed to bring rats with us.

Cockroaches, too, but we didn't have anything to hunt them down except little robot exterminators, and they never quite got the job done.

The door was locked because you locked anything you wanted to keep from getting stolen or vandalized down here, and I didn't have Dog along to hack the system so I had to do it the old-fashioned way.

"Get behind me," I warned Beckett, shielding my face with my right hand and trying to aim my blaster at the magnetic lock plate at an angle where the plasma wouldn't splash back at me.

I slitted my eyes and pulled the trigger. Heat washed over me, sunburn-hot on my neck and hand, and I smelled burnt hair and knew it was mine, but when I looked out from behind my hand, the lock was melted away, a twisted, black mass of metal and plastic, and the door was slowly swinging open. I pushed it open with the barrel of my blaster and held it with my foot, motioning to Beckett.

"Go."

"They're down there!" The words were distant, but I heard them clearly from somewhere past the other end of the alley. "I saw them go this way!"

Beckett's head snapped around at the far-off yell, lips skinned back from her teeth in what might have been fear or anger or both. I pushed gently at her shoulder and she moved through, feeling her way along in the pitch blackness on the other side of the door. I could feel them coming behind us and I wanted to scream at her to hurry so I could get in and get the door closed, but I knew there were stairs inside somewhere and I didn't want to chance pushing her down them, so I waited with patience I do not, generally, have.

When I thought there was enough room, I slipped in beside her and yanked the door shut behind me. It banged far too loudly and I held it in place, knowing it wouldn't lock but hoping to keep it from rebounding and swinging back open. They'd find it eventually, but it would make me feel better if it stayed closed.

I waited for just a moment, hoping my eyes would adjust to the darkness, but the blackness was too deep and there was only so much human rods and cones could do with it. I remembered my night vision glasses hanging in the utility locker and gave myself a mental kick in the butt for neglecting to bring them.

They would have been so much less obtrusive than the flashlight, but at least I'd remembered to bring that with me.

I grabbed it out of the pouch on my gunbelt, slipped my blaster out of its holster and affixed the light to the rail in front of the weapon's trigger before switching it on. Beckett flinched at the sudden flare of white, shielding her eyes and moving back around behind me. A sloped metal ceiling nearly stared me in the face, heading down a staircase only a meter away, its landing bare metal grating beneath our feet. I realized Beckett must have been centimeters from the edge of the first step and I was suddenly glad I hadn't rushed her into the door.

"There's a flashlight on your gunbelt," I told Beckett, moving down the first couple steps to give her room. The ceiling was low, barely two meters of clearance from step to bare, grey metal, and I was glad I wasn't an overly tall man. I started to turn back to the stairs then realized I hadn't been clear. "Don't turn it on yet. Just keep it in your hand in case you need it."

I couldn't see a thing below us except for the flight of stairs we were on and the next landing. The walls were narrow, the ceiling low and the light couldn't penetrate through the gridwork metal more than a few meters.

Good. Get all that between us and whoever's coming behind. Maybe they won't know we came down here.

And I knew that was wishful thinking even before the idea had the chance to bounce from one side of my head to the other, but I kept descending. The metal steps banged and rattled beneath us in a drumline rhythm, far too loud but it couldn't be helped. I leaned against the right-hand railing with my shoulder, the pistol stretched out ahead of me, the light on the steps.

It seemed as if we descended forever, one flight after another, and I'd given up on counting the landings we'd hit or the levels we'd traversed. Exits beckoned at every second landing, and I wondered where they went and if we'd be better off trying one of them. I thought about it, thought about how we'd be stuck down at the lowest levels with no way out. I could use my 'link to find a way back up, and hope we could avoid detection until we reached the Communications Center...

What was it my trainer in the Academy had said?

"Hope in one hand and shit in the other and see which one fills up first."

That reward for our heads was going to be a wildfire devouring the good sense of every gangbanger and wannabe badass all over El Mercado. If we jumped out of one of those doors into the middle of a neighborhood full of innocent bystanders, we'd take the chance of catching them in a crossfire and getting someone killed.

I kept heading downward instead.

"Do you hear that?" Beckett asked, grabbing my shoulder and pulling me up short between one stair and the next.

Annoyance fought for supremacy over exhaustion. I'd fallen into a nice, mind-numbing rhythm that had let me forget how incredibly tired I was, and now I was huffing and puffing and wishing I was anywhere else in the whole galaxy. And I could hear the steps behind us, above us. Still far off, but thumping with the regularity of a heartbeat.

They were coming. I wasn't sure if it was the street muscle or the mercenaries, but someone had found us.

I sucked in a breath, tried to dig up energy from some untapped seam buried inside me but couldn't find any, so I let gravity do the work. At least we were heading down. Relatively speaking of course.

It wasn't too much farther. You couldn't miss the entrance. It was festooned with warnings in every language spoken in the Union and a few that had died off since the station had been constructed, as well as skull and crossbones symbols, radiation warning symbols, heavy machinery warning symbols...well, you get the idea. It was the Lascaux Caves in metal and plastic, and it was locked, of course.

I blasted the door, then had to do it again because I'd flinched the first time and missed the lock plate. I blinked away afterimages and patted bits of white-hot metal off my jacket before they could burn through the lining. Beckett was coughing from the fumes and the only reason I wasn't was that I was still holding my breath. I kicked the door open, the solid impact of my boot sole on four centimeters of solid alloy travelling up my leg and all the way into my back and on into my cracked wrist. I grunted, and then coughed because grunting had made me inhale, and ducked inside with Beckett stumbling close behind.

I turned off my flashlight. I didn't need it in here. Not that it was like sun-bright, but there was a constant background glimmer of pale blue Cherenkov radiation, a sort of nightlight glow that seemed to come from everywhere at once. It traced halos along the curves of endless rows of field generators, dumbbell-shaped columns running from the floor twenty meters up to the ceiling like a redwood forest if the redwood were made of exotic alloys and boron honeycomb composites and carbon nanotubes.

Somewhere in here were control stations, shielded offices with protective suits and battalions of maintenance 'bots, but those weren't kept crewed round the clock. The gravity generators were simple for all that they were nearly a miracle of exotic materials and energy fields no one had even dreamed about until a couple hundred years ago. Not much could go wrong, and the normal parts that wore down and had to be replaced could be handled by the 'bots. We didn't have to worry about the workers finding us or any innocent people getting caught in the crossfire.

"Which way?" Beckett asked, her eyes glazing over a little at the sight of the endless rows of fairy columns.

Good question. One direction looked much like another, so I gestured to the right. I wasn't sure how far we jogged because everything looked the same. There were alphanumeric designators on each of the field generator columns, but not in any sort of order I could discern and nothing to indicate how far we'd gone. I briefly considered trying to make my way to the central power conduit, visible through the forest as a broad, rust-red cylinder at the center of the chamber, nearly a kilometer away, but rejected it. The idea wasn't to give them a landmark where they could find us, it was to blend in.

I went off to our left, about halfway down one of the rows of field generators, equidistant from the central walkway and the outer wall, and dropped to a knee, fighting the urge to lean against one of the glowing columns. I couldn't feel any heat coming off them, couldn't discern any difference from the radiation except for a tingling down my spine that might have been psychological, but I still didn't want to touch them.

Beckett collapsed beside me, sweat pouring off of her, the combined effects of our experiences on Hanuman and here on El Mercado beginning to show in the strain on her face. It probably showed on mine, too, but I didn't have a mirror handy.

"We can just stay here, right?" she said, her breathing rapid enough I began to worry she might hyperventilate. "They wouldn't find us here, would they? We could just wait long enough and they'd leave, right?"

I blew out a sigh, the tail end of catching my breath as well as disappointment in having to tell her the truth.

"Unfortunately, we can't. There's the radiation, and the lack of food and water, and the fact we have to sleep sometime and my arm is only going to get worse…" I shrugged. "You get the idea. I've given them every chance to give up, to leave us alone. And I brought the fight down here where no civilians can get hurt." I felt as if I were trying to talk myself into it more than explaining it to her. "I'm afraid anyone who comes down here, we're just gonna have to kill them."

Beckett didn't react, apparently having no problem with the idea, at least in the abstract.

"Unless they kill us first," I amended. "In which case, our problems will be over."

I grinned. I'd been trying to lighten the mood, but she didn't seem to be taking the joke well. She was staring into space, arms draped across her knees.

"Grant," she said, tentative and quiet, "I need to tell you something."

I waited, letting her get to it in her own time.

"I told you before I didn't have any evidence you could use, but there is something. Something you could take them all down with. If I get killed here…" She trailed off, hissing out a breath, shuddering, but pressed on. "If I get killed, you need to take my body with you."

I scowled.

"Well, that's sort of a macabre request," I said. "This a religious thing, you need to be buried somewhere special or something?"

"Shut up," she snapped. I blinked. She hadn't been that assertive the whole time since I'd met her. "That hopper crash that killed my parents, you read about that, right?"

I nodded. She sucked in a breath before she went on, as if she were having to force this out.

"I was in that hopper with them. I was hurt really bad." Her left hand went to the eye on that side, fingers trailing across her eyelid. "I lost this eye, had some brain damage even."

"Did they grow you a new eye?" I asked her. That would have been standard procedure on Earth or any of the inner colonies, but somewhere like Morrigan, it might have been prohibitively expensive.

"The crash wasn't an accident," she went on as if I hadn't spoken, still not looking at me. "That is, it wasn't just the storm that caused the accident, the automatic guidance system in the hopper was faulty. It was a factory defect, one the company who'd made the system hadn't bothered to correct because it would have cut into their profits more than simply paying for the damages it caused if it ever went wrong."

"Holy...," I trailed off. "That's...someone should have gone to jail for that."

"They might have. Which is why they came to me in the hospital and made me an offer. I didn't have the money for an off-world university, but they said they'd send me to one, then make sure I had a good job afterward." She licked her lips, a nervous sort of motion as if her mouth were dry. "They said they'd take care of me for life, if I let them do one thing. When they replaced my eye, they gave me a new, cutting-edge biomechanical version. Not just cloned tissue, but not bionic either, a combination that would pass most sensor scans." I felt a prickling down my spine, realizing what she was confessing to. I didn't say anything yet, sensing she needed to finish this. "They put a data recorder in the eye. Undetectable. They implanted a computer control for it linked to my optic nerves, with a wireless download capability." She finally met his stare. "They turned me into a ready-made industrial spy and then arranged for me to get the job with Hadur so I could help them take over the company."

Now it was clear why she hadn't told me before. Possession of enhanced bionics by unauthorized civilians was punishable by life in prison or even death. Using the data on the recorder as evidence to clear her of murder and treason would have only got her thrown in jail for the rest of her life for something just as serious. But there was one other question nagging at me, one I had to ask her.

"So, Jake," I said hesitantly. "He didn't know, did he?" She squeezed her eyes shut and tears beaded on her cheeks.

The biomechanical eye can still cry.

"I should have told him. I knew what they were going to do with the company, but I thought…" Shudders went through her. "I thought he'd hate me if he found out. I helped him because I thought maybe I could stop what was happening without them finding out it was me. And I got him killed. It was my fault."

I wanted to comfort her, but I sensed it wouldn't be welcomed right now. Maybe she was too accustomed to self-loathing after all this time. Or if I'm being honest, maybe it was me. Maybe I blamed her for her boyfriend's death the same as she did. She'd known what was happening and she'd let him get himself killed.

"You keep saying 'they' and 'them.' Who?" I shook my head. "Who was behind this? Who gave you the wetware and set all this up? Is it this Nautilus thing? The shell corporation?"

"That's the latest of a dozen names they've gone through just since I was recruited. I don't know what to call them. I only dealt with third parties, lawyers and technicians. But there was one name that came up, not while I was being recruited but when we started looking into Nautilus. I didn't think about it, but you mentioned it before, back in the brothel."

A chill went up my spine and a sense of unreality settled around me that had nothing to do with the gravity field.

"It was Tomas Caty."

[16]

I HAD SO many questions to ask, and suddenly, no time for any of them.

"I think they went this way!"

The shout was heedless, reckless, unprofessional. It was definitely one of the locals we'd seen, not the hit team. A good news-bad news joke. The good news was they weren't the trained squad of corporate mercenaries bent on killing us. The bad news was there were a lot more of them and they could cover more ground than the four remaining assassins could have.

The tap-tap-tap of hard boot soles on the main aisle heading toward us banished my exhaustion and pain with a sudden burst of urgency, and I scrambled to my feet. Shooting at them was a risk, and not just a legal one. I could, conceivably, claim self-defense and not be in much more trouble than I already was. No, the risk was I might miss, probably *would* miss shooting left-handed. I met Beckett's eyes and thought about what lay behind the artificial one. She had proof. She could make things right, which was all I'd ever wanted. Me living through it wasn't necessary.

"Stay here," I told her. "I'm going to draw them off, get them coming after me. Once I do, I want you to get to the Communications Center and call the Marshals. Give them my name, tell them what's going on. Maybe…" I was searching for something to give her hope, trying not to just think of my own goals. "If you're straight with them, if you offer to give up your evidence and testify, I think they'll cut you a deal. Even with the eye. It's better than you'll get from Nautilus."

"Grant," she said, her voice hardly a whisper, her eyes wide with fear. For one of us, though which I wasn't sure. "If you go out there, you're going to get killed."

I shrugged.

"I've pretty much been going to get killed since my wife and son left," I admitted, figuring now was as good a time as any to be completely honest with her and myself. "This seems like as good a way as any."

I took off, sprinting towards the end of the row, toward the voices, not giving her a chance to try to talk me out of it. I *wanted* to be talked out of it, and I was afraid if I gave her too much time, she'd come up with a reason not to do it that I could live with.

Cheer up. Death can't hurt that much.

There were five or six of them coming up the central aisle, spread out on both sides between twenty and a hundred meters away, carefully checking each row of gravity generator nodes, sawed-off shotguns held low and casual like they'd used them before and weren't too worried about any opposition.

Morons. There wouldn't be that big of a price on my head if I weren't dangerous.

My hand was shaking, though not from fear. Pain, exhaustion, adrenaline jitters, yes, all those, but not fear. I couldn't take the time to stop in the middle of the aisle and steady myself, so I settled on spraying and praying, holding down the gun's trigger and hosing the bursts of plasma energy in the general direction of the bad guys. I hit one, miraculously, a thick-chested man with a sculpted brown beard. He squawked and dropped his gun, the stamped metal of the shotgun receiver clattering against the metal grating floor as it hit just a half-second before he did. He continued writhing and screaming once he reached the deck, not dead but not in any shape to get up and join the fun.

If the idea had been to get their attention, well…mission accomplished. Three shotguns roared at once, the reports blending into a rolling thunderclap echoing wildly through the forest of gravity nodes and something smacked into my right shoulder hard enough to make it go numb. I grunted and half-spun with the impact, my left hand and the blaster it held going to the ragged hole in my jacket. The buckshot hadn't penetrated the armor plating beneath the vat-grown leather. I didn't *think* it had, anyway. But they'd seen me and I was fairly confident they'd follow when I ran.

I turned and sprinted away from them. Well, it was more like a shuffling, awkward jog-run, favoring my right side, but it was the best I could manage. I was fairly confident I could string them out, get them all heading past where Beckett was hiding and give her a clear shot at doubling back and finding an exit.

I was sure of that right up to the moment when one of the business-suited corporate mercenaries stepped into the middle of the central aisle only twenty meters ahead of me, a compact blaster pointed at my head. For all my acceptance of the possibility of dying, I still dove out of the way, nearly falling over my feet in a lunge to the right, trying to put gravity node generators between me and the hitman. I stumbled and went down to one knee, twisting around to look back at the mercenary. It was one of the males, tall and spindly with a face like a hatchet blade and how in the living hell he'd managed to get behind us I had no idea.

Of course, you do. The people on the street called them and told them where we were.

And yet these idiots didn't seem to understand who he was or why he was there. The shotguns thundered again, but this time they were shooting at the hitman. I could see the lapels of his dress jacket jump where the buckshot hit, though he didn't even flinch at the shot, just scowled and stood sideways, angling his body in the stance of an ancient duelist, exposing as little of his cross-section as possible as he raised his blaster and fired it back into the El Mercado gangsters.

When I'd been a cop, I'd had to turn down gifts offered to me more than once, but now I was a bounty hunter and this gift was just too nice to pass up. I raised my weapon one-handed and fired, again counting on quantity over quality, pressing the trigger down and keeping it down until the energy pack ran dry. Unfortunately, this guy wasn't some stupid gang-banger with no experience in real gunfights. The minute the blaster flashed sun-bright plasma his way, the hitman was moving.

I wouldn't say he was the fastest man I ever saw, but if not, he was a close second. He jerked backwards out of my line of fire like someone had snagged him with a hook, and most of the energy beam splashed against the closest of the gravity nodes.

I found out in that very moment why shooting gravity generator nodes with a blaster pistol was contraindicated. The casing on the side of the column ruptured quite spectacularly and suddenly there was light and heat and a concussive wave of pure gravity crushing me to the floor like an elephant had planted itself right on top of my chest.

I think I blacked out for a second, but I couldn't be sure. The light switched off and then back on again, and whether it was from me passing out, my eyes being forced shut by instinct, or maybe the interior lighting flickering from the power surge I will never know. When the light came back, the pressure wave was gone and I sucked in an agonized breath. Knives sliced into my chest when it expanded with air and I felt fairly certain even through the haze of possible concussion that I had cracked one or two ribs.

I didn't know if that was *all* I had done, and I didn't want to move until I was sure, but I hurt all over like someone had been beating me with a baseball bat, and it was difficult to differentiate one pain from another. I tried to force my eyes to focus and thought I was in serious trouble when the world seemed to be cloudy and uncertain, until I realized it was merely the effects of the cloud of white smoke hanging over me, swirling with the air currents. More smoke curled off my jacket and my face stung as if I'd been standing out in the sun for a few hours.

My only consolation was that the hitman had gotten it worse. When I was a kid, the frogs used to swarm across the roads after a heavy rain, and at night, the automated cargo trucks would run them over by the score, leaving them flattened, barely recognizable. The hitman could have been one of those frogs. He was squashed just as flat as a human body could be compressed, his blood splashed backwards in a random splatter akin to an ancient style of painting I'd seen in art class in school.

Gravity was a wonderful servant but a terrible, unforgiving master. I'd only received a taste of the edge of the overload burst of gravitons, but the corporate mercenary had taken the full force. I pushed myself up on my left elbow, trying to get my feet beneath me, trying to steady myself despite the world spinning around me, hoping it was just residual dizziness rather than some localized gravitational effect.

The gravity field node was a shattered skeleton, its casing shredded, its base twisted and warped and I just hoped to *God* I didn't have to pay to replace the thing. The nodes around it were charred black but basically intact and so was I, I decided after a brief inventory of my body. I mean, except for the broken wrist and a cracked rib, I was intact. And the possible concussion. And the second degree burns on my face.

Shit. Okay, I was on my feet and ambulatory and grateful for it. I hunted around for my gun and became very annoyed when I couldn't find it. It had been right there in my hand when the blast wave hit. I hadn't been tossed anywhere, so why would it be...

Oh.

Apparently, I'd dropped it when I fell and it had taken a bad bounce right into the path of the pressure wave that had wiped out the hitman. The blaster was twisted into a funky modern-art sculpture sort of thing you might find at ten times scale in front of one of those high-end museums.

Two blasters in one day. And I'd *liked* both those guns.

I was feeling so sorry for myself, I limped out into the central aisle and almost got shot. Only the smoke and steam still floating across the corridor, obscuring me from view, kept me from getting nailed right in the chest with the blaster bolt. It crackled through the haze of smoke, lightning bolts of static electricity arcing away from it, and I lunged back behind cover, knowing exactly who it was. I couldn't see them clearly, but I'd seen a shadowy form short and slender enough it had to be the woman.

A wave of fiery pain radiated from my right arm and left chest, the cost of moving quickly, but I fell into a shuffling jog, another blaster shot encouraging me to keep up the pace. Where were the other two? Were they with her or were they circling around me, trying to cut me off? Or did they already have Beckett and were taking her away while they'd left little Susie Thrillkiller to take care of me?

I was moving painfully slow and felt sure she was going to find me before I made it to the outer wall and the walkway there. I glanced to the side, wondering if I could climb between the field generator nodes and skip over to the next row, but it seemed awfully narrow and offered far too many chances to snag clothes on it. There were also some pretty big stickers on the side of each of the nodes warning of the dangers of touching two of them at the same time and completing an electromagnetic circuit, though that might just have been a liability thing. Either way, I decided to hold off on the idea for the time being, since just keeping myself shuffling forward was taking all the energy I had.

The far wall called to me with visions of alternate exits, storage closets, maybe even tools I could use as weapons, but it was farther away than it looked, or else I was going slower than I thought. The soles of my boots were scraping the floor with each step and I couldn't make myself pick up my feet to stop it. Gravity was pulling at me hard and it had nothing to do with malfunctioning field generators and everything to do with a malfunctioning Grant Masterson. I'd pushed it just about as far as I could without some sleep and some food. And water. Just the thought of water made me realize how thirsty I was and, simultaneously, how badly I had to go to the bathroom. Funny, the things you think about when you're running for your life from a hired killer.

Sweat was pouring down my forehead, stinging my eyes, and I wiped it away with an impatient swipe of my forearm across my face. When I looked up, it seemed as if the far wall had leapt forward, close enough I could see details, like a series of motivational posters taped up at eye level, a flat-screen display built into the wall running some sort of safety lecture on a loop...

And a pissed-off-looking corporate mercenary standing in the center of the aisle, handgun raised up to shoulder level, just waiting for me to get close enough for a nice, easy kill shot. I skidded to a halt, turning back the other way, but stopped again so abruptly I nearly fell over. The woman was behind me, only thirty meters away, her own pistol raised and ready to shoot.

This was it, end of the line. The guy was closer and, anachronistic as it was, I hated the idea of punching a woman, even one trying to kill me, so I decided to rush him. It was all academic because I never would have reached either one of them before they shot me down, but you have to occupy yourself somehow when you're about to die.

I took a step toward the man…and kept going. The pressure came off my ribs and my wrist, and my stomach began doing flip-flops in a way it only did on those rare occasions when I was in free-fall. This was one of those rare occasions. The momentum from my one step hadn't carried me very far, just a couple meters off the ground before the air currents from overhead began spinning me around. I had no anchor, nothing to grab until my hand brushed one of the gravity generation nodes and I caught hold by instinct.

I thought something dire was about to happen to me, something like the brightly-colored alarmist warnings on the safety posters, but there was a qualitative difference between the generator node now from when I'd first entered the chamber, a sound or possibly a feeling missing from it. I knew instinctively from the feel of the metal that it had been deactivated. Or perhaps it was the general lack of gravity informing my instincts. I'm not sure. I had a concussion, you know?

The mercenaries didn't have concussions or excuses, but they both seemed just as nonplused by the zero gravity, and neither was close enough to any of the node columns to get a hold on it and pull themselves back to the floor. I was closer to the man, better able to see the consternation on his face. He was a slicked-back, too-handsome type, probably a big hit with the bar girls—or boys—in places like El Mercado. He looked unused to being out of control and his arms were flailing, the blaster in his hand seemingly forgotten as he tried, and failed, to move himself in any direction at all.

Which was why I was only half a meter off the surface while the two mercenaries were four meters up and swimming help-lessly in mid-air when the gravity came back with a vengeance. I was suddenly falling onto my butt and *barely* had the wherewithal to slap my left hand out and spread the impact before my shoulders struck the floor, which would have done nasty things to my cracked ribs. It wasn't exactly pleasant, anyway, and while I couldn't have sworn to it, I thought the gravity had gone over standard by at least half again.

The mercenaries might have agreed if they hadn't been too busy screaming. My ears had been ringing from the fall, and from the sudden yo-yo jerking back and forth of gravitational pull, but I'd still heard the smack of flesh onto the bare floor, the unmistakable crunch of breaking bones.

The woman had made the mistake of trying to put an arm out to stop her fall. Rookie move. Any decent martial arts class will teach you how to fall first, before almost anything else. And the first rule is, *don't* put your hands out. You'll wind up with broken fingers, a broken wrist or maybe even, as in this case, a compound fracture of your right arm.

Her suit jacket was made of some durable stuff and the bone hadn't ripped through it, but there was a lump pressed against the sleeve and I'd seen it enough times before to recognize the signs. The woman had never been hurt bad before. You can tell when someone is in real, intense pain for the first time ever. They hit shock a lot quicker than people who've been there before and know the drill. She was out of the fight, her eyes glazing over, sweat beading on her chocolate skin and shivers running through her shoulders, and I was fairly sure she was about to pass out.

The guy, he was in worse shape physically. I winced and fought an instinct to look away when I saw his left leg bent the wrong way, tucked back under his body. He was screaming but he wasn't about to pass out, worse luck for him. He'd dropped his blaster and I hobbled over to him, wheezing at the agony in my chest. I had to go to a knee to pick up the weapon, unable to bend over for fear I'd simply black out on the way down.

Once I had the gun in my hand, I backed away from him,

toward the far wall of the chamber, only now having the luxury of wondering how in the hell that had happened.

Man, if I live through this, I just have *to start watching my language again. I'm falling into old habits.* Janie hadn't liked me swearing. She'd made me promise to stop after Luke was born.

Something squeezed at my chest, but it wasn't the pain from my ribs. I should have known better than to let myself get emotional when I was in pain and vulnerable. Too easy to lose control and get all weepy. I didn't have time for that now.

"Grant, are you okay?"

For a hazy, senseless moment, I had the mad notion it was Janie coming up behind me, asking the question in such a solicitous, tender voice, just like before. Then I blinked the tears away and recognized Delia Beckett.

"How'd you get over here?" I asked her, frowning. "You were supposed to run, get away."

She grabbed my shoulder and tried to support me and I had to wince and pull away.

"I couldn't let you die for me," she insisted. "Not after Jake."

"The gravity," I deduced. "That was you?"

She nodded.

"There's a series of maintenance panels in the wall back over there." She hooked a thumb over her shoulder. "I guess they don't expect anyone to break in here and mess with anything, because their encryption is for shit." She sighed heavily. "Unfortunately, they have fail-safes that kicked in after I did it and it locked down all the controls."

She'd probably just sent the gravity surge all the way up through every level of the station, and I hoped no one else had been hurt by it. No one who didn't deserve it.

"Thanks. Let's get out of here before either of them works enough energy up to try something stupid and make me kill them."

"Which way?"

Good question.

One way seemed as good as another and there were exit signs at either end of the chamber, plus the one we'd come through to get here. I didn't want to go back through that one because the odds were, either the hit squad or the street gangers had left someone there waiting for us.

"Let's try this way," I nodded the way I was facing since it would hurt less than turning around.

It turned out to be the wrong decision. We hadn't made it a half a dozen steps before someone else was shooting at us. I didn't hear the gunshots, not at first. Something rammed into my back and I was suddenly on the ground, hot knives from the edges of broken ribs slicing through my chest, a roaring in my ears drowning out everything else. Beckett was pressing against my side, turning every breath, every second into relentless torture and I tried to scream at her to move but I didn't have the breath for it.

It took me several seconds to realize the roaring wasn't just the pain, it was gunfire. Buckshot ricocheted off the gravity nodes in a hand-bell choir of metallic clinks and clanks and a stray round caromed off the floor only centimeters from my head. They were getting close and I couldn't even see them, not with Beckett pinning me to the ground. I'd dropped the blaster when she hit me and I couldn't see it either and I knew they'd be getting closer.

It cost me screaming agony in my chest, but I pushed Beckett off of me and rolled over, ready to yell at her for not getting to cover until I felt the tacky wetness beneath my left hand. She'd been shot. Her face was a ghostly white, and blood coated the right side of her shirt. She tried to breathe and coughed instead, red flecks of frothy blood staining her chin. She'd taken a round through one of her lungs.

I could still save her, I just had to get her out of here, get her to a medic.

Another volley of gunshots, spiteful cracks not as deep as the shotgun blasts. Someone had a handgun, small caliber most likely. I threw myself over Beckett, trying to shield her body with mine, knowing my armored jacket would stop the rounds, and started hunting around to find the blaster.

I should have kept my eyes on the floor, kept searching for the gun, but I was only human and I let myself glance up at the enemy for just a second. There were five of them, all men, all the gang-bangers we'd seen on the street, the ones who'd followed us down the stairs. They'd circled around the other end of the chamber and outflanked us while we'd been tangled up fighting the mercenaries.

Their faces were masks of avarice, not seeing us, not seeing the bleeding, helpless woman and the beat-up, useless ex-Marshal, just seeing the money they'd get for heads on a platter. They advanced in a loose wedge, not from any tactical training I was certain, but just to keep from accidentally shooting each other. The leader, the point of the arrowhead, was the one with the pistol, dull, stamped metal fabricated on some illegal machine off a black market pattern. He held it sideways, ignoring the sights. Only twenty or thirty meters away and they still weren't hitting us yet. They couldn't shoot for shit, but they were willing to get as close as they needed.

I had to find that blaster…

Lightning flashed out of the periphery of my vision, streaking across from right to left and punching through the chest of the man with the pistol. He'd been wearing a thick, black duster, probably armored, but not nearly enough to stop the blaster shot. A brief flare of burning cloth and sublimating ceramic plating, a puff of black smoke and a spray of blood and the gang leader was toppling over, felled like a redwood.

The others stopped in their tracks, faces frozen in shock, shot-guns raised halfway up to chest level.

"Drop the fucking guns or you're dead, assholes!"

The bellow was tinged with a familiar, slightly plaintive tone I would have recognized anywhere.

"Larry?" I murmured, trying to twist around the other direction and gritting my teeth against the pain the movement caused.

The gang-bangers dropped their shotguns slowly, the weapons clattering one at a time against the metal grating of the floor, hands going up. Two squads of blue-armored Union Marshals rushed in at the signal of surrender, blaster carbines levelled and ready to take out anyone who moved.

My mouth hung open and for just a moment, I forgot about the pain in my chest and the wounded civilian beside me and stared. I was still staring when Larry Daniels stepped in front of me, his weapon tucked under his arm, an "I told you so" expression on his chiseled face beneath his tactical helmet.

"You're gonna get yourself killed, Grant," he said, kneeling down so I didn't have to crane my neck up to look at him. "You know that, right?"

"She needs help," I said, unable to come up with anything more intelligent, waving toward Beckett. She was unconscious now, but still struggling to breathe. "She's been shot."

"Medic!" Larry yelled behind him. "Get up here, it's secure!"

Two more Marshals in blue, a red cross marking their bulky armor plating, slid in beside Beckett, quickly and expertly stripping off bloody clothing and applying smart bandages. I let out a sigh, knowing she would make it now. They'd take care of her. Relieved of the burden of her survival, my mind went back to my own injuries and I very nearly passed out.

"See to him when you're done with that one," Larry told the medics, and I thought I heard real concern in his tone.

"I'm damned glad you're here, Larry," I said, my voice coming out a pained wheeze. "But how the hell did you find us? We never did get to send out a distress call."

Larry didn't answer, just nodded off to the right. Coming up behind the medics, limping on three legs, the hair on his rear flanks charred and blackened, grinning in a way that was very canine and yet so very human as well, was Dog.

I tried to say something coherent and again, failed.

"You were...," I started, tripping over the words. "How did..."

"I told you I had to do some self-repair," he said, tilting his head in a shrug. "Once I got the power feed issue taken care of, it wasn't that hard to slip out of the docking bay. No one looks at a robot, even a damaged one."

"Grant," Larry told me, his eyes set in grim accusation, "you've got complaints filed against you from Morrigan to Hanuman to here, from Traffic Control, local law enforcement, corporate security.... And then there's *this*," he said, gesturing at Dog. "Buddy, you've got some serious explaining to do."

"Yeah," I acknowledged, feeling everything start to spin around me, the cumulative effect of exhaustion, dehydration and maybe a little internal bleeding finally beginning to take their toll. "But not right now."

I passed out.

$$[\ 17\ ]$$

"You look a lot better now than the last time I saw you."

Delia Beckett paused in packing the small shoulder bag and turned as I entered the room. It wasn't quite a hospital room, wasn't exactly a jell cell, but reminded me of both. The uniformed Marshal standing in the hallway just outside the open door made it seem more the latter.

"Same to you, cowboy," she said, smirking at the Stetson. I'd retrieved it from the *Charietto* after the Marshals had hauled it here to Government Central, not wanting to leave it in case the feds wound up confiscating the ship. Of course, they might still throw me in jail, but one thing at a time.

"Aw, I just had a couple broken ribs." I waved it away with a wrist that had been swollen to twice its size only a couple days ago. "Nothing a little time in the bone growth stimulator couldn't make short work of. You saved my life. Twice."

No point in mentioning I could have survived the shot she'd taken for me. It was the thought that counted.

"And all I did was bring trouble your way," I reflected, speaking the words that had been gnawing at me for a while now.

"You were doing fine living there in Absolution and I screwed everything up for you."

She zipped the bag shut and slung it over her shoulder, laughing softly.

"I was dying inside a little bit every day back on Morrigan. Someone would have found me eventually. I wasn't trying too hard to stay hidden. This way…" She motioned around her. "This way at least I can start trying to make it right."

"They must really want what you had in those implant data crystals," I mused, shaking my head. "Total immunity and witness protection…the Marshals don't throw that sort of deal around much."

"They deactivated the implant," she said with an indifferent shrug. "It's been grown over with nerve tissue and there's no safe way to replace it, so I'm going to be blind in one eye, but it seems a small price to pay for what I've done."

"It's a fresh start," I said. "Most people don't get that chance." I shrugged. "Trust me, I know."

"I get to go be a rehab therapist on some outer colony." She stepped closer. She seemed cleaner now, less haggard, younger even. I decided I didn't feel so guilty anymore. "But what do you get?"

"I'm about to find out." I pointed a thumb back at the hallway. "I go meet with the Chief Inspector in like five minutes. I just wanted to make sure to say goodbye first. I've never been very good at saying goodbye. When my dad died, I didn't even want to go to the funeral. It felt like it wouldn't be real if I didn't say goodbye."

"This doesn't have to be quite that final, I hope. But if it is, maybe you should try to do what you helped me to do."

She wrapped me in a hug and I returned it a bit awkwardly. I've never been much of a hugger.

"Forgive yourself," she told me.

I've never been big on that, either.

"I'll try," I promised.

And then she followed the guard out of the room and down the corridor, and she was gone. It was my turn to face my fate. At least they hadn't kept me under guard since I was released from the medical ward. Heck, they hadn't even stuck me in the inmate section, which I'd very much appreciated. Of course, they hadn't let me see Dog, either, and I suppose they'd known I wouldn't try to run without him.

The walk was long and there were stares this time, but not the resentful kind, and I wondered just how much everyone knew about what had happened. It was also possible they were staring at my hat. You didn't see many Stetsons in a Union Marshals' headquarters, except on Halloween.

Larry was waiting for me in front of Tanaka's office, arms folded and an expression of disbelief on his face.

"How did you do it, Masterson?" he asked, no resentment in his tone just a sort of awe-filled skepticism. "How did you turn this fuck-up into one of the biggest busts in the history of this base? Do you know how many judges we had to roust from their beds to write up the warrants before the word got out? How many strike teams we had to send out to raid the corporate headquarters of Hadur, BramCo and a half a dozen others? My God, we've made more arrests in the last three days than we have in the last year!"

"It's a gift, Larry," I said, spreading my hands. "Consider it my way of saying thanks for pulling my fat out of the fire."

"Felt like old times." He offered a hand and I shook it. It did feel like old times. "Good luck in there," he said, reaching over to knock on Tanaka's door for me.

"Come." Her voice was curt in a familiar way I hadn't realized I'd missed.

I gave Larry a final nod, pulled off my hat and walked into the office. It was sparsely, almost Spartanly decorated, the only thing unrelated to Tanaka's career a small holo-cube cycling photos and videos of her husband and children on a loop. The Chief Inspector was behind her desk, leaning back in her chair and watching me with the keen expression of a hawk circling a field mouse. The door slammed shut behind me and I glanced back at it sharply, only then noticing Dog sitting on the floor beside Tanaka's desk.

He was, I saw, completely repaired, right down to the fur on his haunches.

"They wouldn't let me see you," Dog said plaintively, then fell silent at Tanaka's glare.

Holy hell, she can even shut Dog up.

"Please sit down, Mr. Masterson," she said, motioning at the chair across from her.

There was only one chair, sturdy and comfortable with padded faux leather that creaked beneath my weight as I settled into it. I'd been in her office before with others and there was always just the right number of chairs for however many people were in her office at the time. It was uncanny.

"We are faced with an interesting situation here, Mr. Masterson," she said, hands folded in front of her, elbows resting on the desktop. "Between what Ms. Beckett provided for us from her implant and the records your..." She paused, her mouth hardening in disapproval. "...your *dog* here uploaded from the lab on Hanuman, we have been able to identify a senior Union Representative, Tomas Caty, as being involved in a smuggling ring dealing in black-market military-grade Bartoli crystals and illegal human experimentation."

She pushed up from the desk and paced restlessly behind it, hands clasped at the small of her back, a lion trapped in a cage.

"Right now, we have enough to arrest him and make a fair case in court." She stopped in mid-stride to shrug. "Not insurmountable, but enough to ruin his career, certainly. But he'd be the end of it, unless we were willing to cut him a deal to get to the next rung up on the ladder."

"What makes you so certain he's not the top rung, ma'am?" I asked her.

She scowled at me as if I should know better.

"Caty is *not* intelligent enough to pull something this far-ranging off on his own. He's a politician's politician, an expert at charm and glad-handing and talking out of both sides of his mouth. I'd be willing to bet my pension he's someone's sock-puppet." She turned a hand over demonstratively. "Which means he might take us up on that deal, but Goddammit, Grant, I don't want to give him one. He doesn't deserve to come out of this Scot-free, not after what he did to you."

I could sense all this leading to something, and since I'd never known Maggie Tanaka to beat around the bush before, I could tell it was something she didn't like.

"Come on, ma'am," I urged. "Out with it."

"The thing is, Grant, with what we have now, if we do cut a deal with Caty, we could get him to confess that the evidence he presented of you bugging his offices was doctored. You could be reinstated, get it all back within weeks."

Okay. *Now* I understood.

I sank back into the chair and let my head tilt back, eyes on the ceiling, imagining being back on the job. I noticed Dog hadn't said anything, and I wondered if he was that impressed by Tanaka or if he was being reticent because he wanted me to think about what was important to me instead of him.

Which would be giving him credit for a lot more grace and selflessness than he'd ever demonstrated before.

If I had my job back, if I was cleared of all charges, I could even get visitation rights with Luke. It wouldn't be often unless I could get reassigned to the Solar System, but not-often was still better than never.

"What's the alternative, Chief?"

"The alternative is, you leave her with your ship fixed and your bounty paid and your *companion*." She glared again at Dog. "And you continue acting as a bounty hunter with no official support from the Marshals or anyone in the government…but *unofficially*, you'll be acting on information I give you and helping us follow leads into whoever is behind Nautilus."

"What do you know about them?" I asked, trying to buy time so I wouldn't have to give my answer yet.

"Not enough. We think it has its fingers in dozens of criminal enterprises and is heavily involved in the Evolutionist Cult."

My ears pricked up at that. The Evolutionists thought cybernetics were the next step in human development and financed their criminal use of enhanced bionics through smuggling and murder for hire.

"We've been investigating them for the better part of a year, but every time we've tried to send a Marshal in undercover, they've been burned." Her expression hardened. "A couple have wound up dead, no suspects, no explanation." She emerged from behind the desk and put a hand on my arm. I stared at it for a moment, wondering if it was a prelude to violence. "Grant, I can't ask you to do this. Not officially. But if I know you, I don't have to, do I?"

———

"So," Dog said, settling into the copilot's seat, resting a paw on the console, "where to next?"

I enjoyed the feel of my seat on the *Charietto* in silence for just a moment. Would I have really given her up, given Dog up, for the chance to go back to my old life?

"Tanaka gave me a lead about a fugitive out in the Paragon at

Barnard's Star. Muscle for a big-time smuggler who was linked through Nautilus to Caty in the data you scooped up."

I turned to him and grinned.

"We're going hunting."

———

The story continues in Book 2, Resolution.

THANK YOU FOR READING ABSOLUTION

WE HOPE you enjoyed it as much as we enjoyed bringing it to you. We just wanted to take a moment to encourage you to review the book. Follow this link: Absolution to be directed to the book's Amazon product page to leave your review.

Every review helps further the author's reach and, ultimately, helps them continue writing fantastic books for us all to enjoy.

———

You can also join our non-spam mailing list by visiting www. subscribepage.com/AethonReadersGroup and never miss out on future releases. You'll also receive three full books completely Free as our thanks to you.

Facebook | Instagram | Twitter | Website

Want to discuss our books with other readers and even the

authors? Join our Discord server today and be a part of the Aethon community.

ALSO IN SERIES:
Absolution
Retribution
Revolution

Drafted into a private army, he must fight monsters... or be hunted as one... A century after the Break destroyed much of the world, the wealthy island nation of Dios stands alone as a paradise for those than remain... so long as they aren't poor and homeless. For street orphan Grant Riven, life is a series of kicks to the face. Until exposure to a powerful mutating agent gives him super strength, passive-regeneration, and the ability to use powerful weapons. The downside? Lots of other people have mutated as well, except they're insane and want to eat everyone. After he's recruited by Cloud Nine Engineering, the most powerful corporation in Dios, Grant is labeled "Hallowed"–the fancy name for his new mutation–and drafted into a war against the Mutes, the cannibalistic mutants overrunning Dios. The deal is simple. In exchange for risking his life to fight monsters, Cloud Nine will provide him with the cure that keeps him from becoming a monster himself.

GET SPACE JUNK NOW!

Dillon Mackey has always wanted to travel the stars...
When brilliant scientist and inventor Sherisza Rousilarru
offers him an apprenticeship aboard her starship, he leaps at
the chance to escape a boring future in the law. But she's not
the last of her kind for no reason. Dillon finds himself
caught up in intrigue and adventure across systems, empires,
and alien worlds he'd only dreamt of ever seeing. Just what
other secrets does his reclusive mentor hide? And will being
her apprentice make him a target of her enemies?

GET ESCAPING GRAVITY NOW!

"Aliens, agents, and espionage abound in this Cold War-era alternate history adventure... A wild ride!"—Dennis E. Taylor, bestselling author of We Are Legion (We Are Bob)

GET THE LUNA MISSILE CRISIS NOW!

For all our Sci-Fi books, visit our website.